She stared at him in frozen outrage

"I don't know what you're trying to imply," Tamara said furiously, "but if you're suggesting I came here deliberately looking for you, Mr. Fletcher, you couldn't be more wrong. You see," she told Zach sweetly, raising her left hand, "I don't happen to need to run after other men—I've already managed to catch mine! And if I'd known you'd come here," she finished with a flourish, "I would have made a point of avoiding it."

"Would you have, indeed?" Zach's eyes were on her left hand, narrowed and faintly assessing. "Are you sure about that? Women have been known to do strange things when deprived of their fiancés' presence."

PENNY JORDAN
is also the author of these

Harlequin Presents

Many of these books are available at your local bookseller.

For a free catalog listing all titles currently available,
send your name and address to:

HARLEQUIN READER SERVICE
1440 South Priest Drive, Tempe, AZ 85281
Canadian address: Stratford, Ontario N5A 6W2

PENNY JORDAN

escape from desire

Harlequin Books

TORONTO • NEW YORK • LOS ANGELES • LONDON
AMSTERDAM • PARIS • SYDNEY • HAMBURG
STOCKHOLM • ATHENS • TOKYO • MILAN

Harlequin Presents first edition February 1983
ISBN 0-373-10569-X

Original hardcover edition published in 1982
by Mills & Boon Limited

CHAPTER ONE

TAMARA sat up slowly, pushing a heavy swathe of wheat blonde hair back off her face. She didn't normally wear it down, and already the hot Caribbean sun was beginning to bleach the loose wisps on her forehead silver. Cool grey eyes gazed thoughtfully out of a high-cheekboned, oval face of almost classical perfection, their expression faintly withdrawn, wary almost. It was Tamara's habitual expression and one which had attracted the interest of more than one predatory male, until they realised that with Tamara the cool façade was more than merely skin-deep.

From the beach the sound of merrymaking and laughter was borne towards her on the light tropical breeze; from the swimming pool she could hear splashes and high-pitched childish voices, but here in the gardens of the luxurious holiday complex on St Stephen's, there was no interruption and she had their beauty to herself.

She put down her paperback and glanced at her watch. Not long until lunch. The paperback was more of a safeguard against unwanted intruders than a compelling read; that was one of the problems about holidaying alone, but she had had little option—Malcolm hadn't been able to come with her.

Malcolm! Sunlight glinted on the solitaire diamond on her left hand, the stone large enough to reveal its value, and yet not so large that it could ever be described as ostentatious. So typical of Malcolm. Eyebrows several shades darker than her hair drew together in a faint frown, What was the matter with her? Until now she had been perfectly content with Malcolm and their engagement. She sighed pensively. Perhaps it was the atmosphere of this tropical island paradise; or perhaps it had something to do with the fact that the majority of the other guests were young couples, still at the honeymoon stage, or older couples free of growing families for the first time, bent on recapturing the magic of those earlier days. Certainly there were families among the hotel's many guests, but somehow the atmosphere pervading the complex was essentially one of a sensuous lethargy, which was beginning to have its effect on Tamara's thoughts, releasing doubts and breaking down barriers she hadn't even been aware were there.

One of the main reasons she had agreed to marry Malcolm was because of his solid dependability, his lack of imagination and sexual magnetism. That wasn't what she wanted in a husband. In the world of publishing in which she worked, as personal assistant to the fiction editor of a prestigious small publishing firm, she had seen all too often the results of hastily and ill-considered marriages, where two people declared that they had fallen madly in love only to change their minds within six or twelve months. That wasn't for her. She wanted the sort of marriage her parents had had. Her parents. She sighed again, remembering the love and laughter which had pervaded the first fifteen years of her life, but all that love and laughter had gone the night they lost their lives in a motorway pile-up, leaving Tamara to be brought up by her father's aunt, Lilian Forbes. Of course Aunt Lilian had been well-intentioned—it couldn't have been an easy task to be faced with sole responsibility for a fifteen-year-old who was perhaps too emotional for her own good, but she was a distant, unbending woman, unused to children and found it difficult to show the spontaneous affection Tamara had been used to sharing with her parents, so gradually Tamara had learned to conceal behind a cool smile the turmoil of growing up feeling herself unloved and rejected. Eventually she herself, without realising it, had adopted her aunt's mistrust of physically displayed affection, so that the boys she met found her cool and standoffish, turning to other girls less unapproachable and thus reinforcing Tamara's conviction that she lacked the desirability of her peers.

To compensate for this she had pursued a career while other girls in the small village in which she lived got married and had babies, and at twenty-six she now considered herself immune from the emotions which seemed to possess other girls, and had been quite happy to accept Malcolm's proposal.

Not that she had accepted him only for the sake of being married. London was no small village and there were plenty of men alive to the possibilities hidden deep within her cool exterior, but Tamara could never overcome the deep mistrust of what she termed 'charmers', which she had learned from her aunt.

She had even approved of the way in which Malcolm had taken her home to meet his parents, not once but twice, for what she knew to be a 'vetting'. Colonel and Mrs Mellors had been polite but unforthcoming, and Tamara had sensed that they would have preferred to see their son married to one of their own set. Tamara could understand why. Although she had a well paid job and had done well for herself, she did not have the 'county' connections to appeal to the rather snobbish Mellors. Malcolm's father owned and ran a small country estate which Malcolm had told her would come down to him in due course, but for now he was quite content with his accountancy partnership which enabled him to maintain an expensive London flat, and the BMW car he had bought just before their engagement.

Life with Malcolm would be as calm and orderly as drifting down a canal, and suddenly for the first time Tamara wondered if she really wanted such a narrow existence.

Suddenly feeling restless, she got up, and walked towards the beach; a tall slender girl with a cool 'touch me not' air which clung protectively to her.

Through the cluster of palms fringing the silver crescent of sand, Tamara could see one of the couples who had been on the same flight as herself. In their early twenties, and patently on honeymoon, their pleasure in one another was like a tiny piece of grit marring the placid surface of her life, and irritating her into the admission that Malcolm and the marriage they would have was not what her parents would have wanted for her.

The young couple were ducking one another playfully in the water; Malcolm hated any demonstrations of affection in public. What would their honeymoon be like? He had suggested they spent it in the Algarve; his parents had friends who owned a villa there and the golf courses were excellent.

Was that really what she wanted? she wondered; a husband who devoted himself to golf while she played bridge with his friends' wives?

Telling herself that she was being stupidly emotional, Tamara gathered up her belongings prior to changing for lunch. Many people didn't bother, simply eating at the poolside tables dressed completely informally, but Tamara felt after a morning in the intense heat of the tropical sun, her body covered in oil, that she wanted to shower and then eat somewhere where it was cool. She normally tanned well, despite her fair skin, but because she had never been so near the Equator before she was deliberately taking extra care to protect her skin from burning.

The hotel complex was attractive—bungalows for family occupation dotted the grounds, ablaze with jacaranda, bougainvillea, hibiscus, and passion flowers, but she had a room in the hotel itself—a double one, since she had originally been coming away on holiday with another girl from the publishing firm, but she had been transferred to their New York office at short notice and so Tamara had come away alone.

Malcolm had encouraged her. He was rather busy and felt that he himself would be unable to get away until their honeymoon, and as it was almost two years since she had had a proper holiday—her aunt had been very ill for a long time and Tamara had helped to nurse her through her terminal illness, using up all her holiday leave—Tamara had felt that she needed the break.

To get to her room she had to walk through the hotel foyer, a cool, shady room with a terrazzo-tiled floor, cane furniture and plenty of greenery. The receptionist smiled at her as she asked for her key. All the staff were exceptionally pleasant and ready to help. Tamara smiled back, and ran quickly up the flight of stairs leading to the bedrooms.

By law no building on the island could be higher

than two storeys, and it was pleasant to be able to look out of her bedroom window, and to find that the only thing obstructing her view of the Caribbean was a clump of palm trees, waving slightly in the onshore breeze.

As she stripped off her swimsuit Tamara was pleased to see that already her skin was turning a warm honey shade—Malcolm did not approve of bikinis, nor had Aunt Lilian, and Tamara had never owned one. There was a boutique attached to the hotel, and she had noticed some particularly attractive swimwear in the window when she walked past it. Her swimsuit was completely plain—a dull navy, which when compared with the bright beach clothes worn by the other visitors seemed very schoolgirlish and almost frumpish.

The water pressure in the shower could sometimes be erratic, as Tamara had already learned, but today it worked reasonably efficiently, the cool spray delicious against her hot skin.

As she stepped out she caught sight of her naked body in the mirror, her breasts warmly full, but firm, the nipples a delicate pink against the pale flesh. She tried to visualise Malcolm as her husband, the two of them sharing the intimacies of the bedroom, but her imagination refused to conjure up the image. Cross with herself, she pulled a slender cotton dress from the wardrobe, brushing her hair vigorously, and constraining it into a neat knot at the back, before slipping on loose espadrilles.

The dining room was busier than she had anticipated. She had brought her book with her as protection and had hoped to secure one of the smaller tables furthest away from the huge windows overlooking the sea, so that she could eat there unnoticed by the other guests.

This hope was forestalled the moment she entered the restaurant because she was hailed by a plump, dark-haired woman with a friendly smile.

'Tamara! Come and join us.'

She indicated one of the two spare chairs at the table she was sharing with her husband, and Tamara had no option but to slide into one of them, and accept the menu George Partington was handing her.

George and Dot had been on the same flight from Heathrow as Tamara and had introduced themselves to her at the airport. They were an outward-going couple, obviously quick to make friends, and Tamara suspected that, unlike her, they already knew most of their fellow guests.

The hotel was a relatively new one, and had not previously been used by package holiday firms, and consequently only half a dozen or so people on board their flight from Heathrow had had as their final destination, this particular hotel.

Among them had been the honeymooners Tamara had seen on the beach; a foursome, comprising two young couples who tended to stick together; George and Dot; two young girls, Tamara herself and a man who seemed to have come on his own and whom Tamara had glimpsed momentarily at the airport.

'Try the shrimp and avocado salad,' Dot encouraged her. 'It's delicious. Even now after several days I still can't get used to the sight of avocados actually growing!' Her eyes went to Tamara's engagement ring. 'You're here on your own, aren't you?' she asked curiously.

'Yes.'

Tamara felt reluctant to answer any questions about herself and was glad when Dot's attention

was transferred from her to the man just entering
the restaurant.

Dressed in black jeans and a thin black cotton
shirt, he looked sombrely out of place in a room
where most of the men were wearing brightly pat-
terned beach shirts and light-coloured trousers. He
was different in other ways, too, she reflected,
unable to pinpoint exactly why the man standing
by the door should look so unlike any of the other
holidaymakers. A shock of thick dark hair brushed
the collar of his shirt, thick dark lashes concealing
his eyes from her quick scrutiny.

'There's Zachary Fletcher,' Dot murmured to
George. 'Ask him if he wants to join us. Isn't he
devastatingly sexy?' she appealed to Tamara while
George redoubled his efforts to catch the other
man's eye. 'We were talking to him in the bar last
night. Oh, he hasn't seen us!' she exclaimed in dis-
appointment as the other man turned and walked
towards one of the small tables almost hidden away
in a corner of the room.

Even the way he walked was different from other
people. Tamara reflected, aware of a tense watching quality in the way he moved, quickly and in-
credibly quietly for so tall and muscular a man. As
he moved muscles rippled under the thin black
shirt, the fabric of his jeans moving against the taut
pressure of his thighs. Tamara found that she was
holding her breath, studying the harshly chiselled
features of a face that gave absolutely nothing
away; a hard, too cynical face for a man who at
most could only be in his mid-thirties.

'Devastatingly sexy', Dot had called him, and
on a wave of revulsion Tamara acknowledged that
the older woman was right. The man exuded a
sensuality which was quite unmistakable. There

wasn't a woman in the room who had not watched him covertly as he walked across it, and Tamara felt almost sickened by their, and her own, avid interest in a man so patently uninterested in them.

He barely raised his eyes from the table except to order his meal, and Tamara noticed that his right arm hung a little awkwardly.

'He's here to recuperate from an accident,' Dot told her excitedly, adding in a confiding tone, 'He's in the Army—oh, he didn't tell us that, but I couldn't help noticing it on his passport as we came through Customs.'

Tamara glanced at him again, convinced that Dot must have made a mistake. He didn't strike her as the type of man who would accept the tight discipline of the Army—unlike Colonel Mellor, Malcolm's father, whose considered opinion it was that Modern Youth badly needed a spell of 'square bashing'—he looked like a loner, a man who deliberately withdrew himself from the pack. And that thick long hair didn't suggest the Army either. He lifted his head, catching her off guard, cool green eyes surveying her with devastating intensity, before she was released, trembling inwardly, from the laser beam of his searching glance.

After they had finished their lunch Tamara accompanied the Partingtons back through the hotel foyer, lingering with Dot over the window display in the boutique.

'Won't you just look at that bikini!' Dot sighed, pointing out the briefest scraps of cyclamen pink cotton Tamara had ever seen in her life. 'If only I had a figure like yours! Why don't you go in and try it on?' she urged, her eyes twinkling as she added, 'Treat yourself and your fiancé.'

'Oh, I couldn't!'

'Of course you could. I'll come with you, George can wait outside.'

Like it or not, Tamara was propelled inside the boutique, Dot telling the attractive dark-skinned girl who stepped forward to serve them that they wanted to see the bikini in the window.

'It's French,' the girl explained in a soft voice. 'And the colour will look stunning with your hair. I think you'll find it's your size. There's a changing cubicle just behind the curtain.' She indicated to the rear of the boutique and Tamara went reluctantly towards it, wishing she had had the strength of will to refuse to enter the shop in the first place, but there was no overruling Dot without actually being rude, and Tamara liked the older woman too much to want to do that.

While she stripped and changed into the brief triangles of cotton she could hear Dot explaining to the salesgirl that she and George were enjoying a silver wedding anniversary present to themselves.

'With both our children married and their own lives to lead we decided it was now or never—before the grandchildren start to arrive,' Tamara heard her say as she fastened the strings of the minute briefs and stared at herself in the mirror.

Her skin gleamed silkily in the half-light of the changing cubicle, almost translucent where the sun hadn't touched it. The bikini top cupped the soft swell of her breasts, the clever stitching shaping them so that her body seemed to have a voluptuousness she didn't recognise.

'Are you ready in there?'

She stepped reluctantly out of the cubicle, feeling selfconscious and awkward, wishing for the first time since she had left her teens behind that she wasn't quite so tall. She felt as though she were exposing an almost indecent length of leg, and longed for a wrap or something similar to provide her with a little more protection than that afforded by the minute scraps of cotton.

'Oh, Tamara, you look fantastic!' Dot exclaimed admiringly. 'You must buy it. You'll really stun them on the beach in that!'

'Don't you think it's a little bit...' Tamara searched for the words to describe her doubts, but Dot waved them aside.

'It's lovely,' she declared stoutly. 'You should be proud of your attractive body, my dear, not ashamed of it. Wait until that fiancé of yours sees you in it!'

'I don't think Malcolm would approve,' Tamara told her faintly, surprised to see the frown suddenly creasing Dot's forehead.

When the salesgirl moved away to answer the telephone Dot said firmly to Tamara, 'You can tell me that it's no business of mine if you like—after all, we have only just met, but I believe in always speaking my mind—it saves a deal of worry and trouble in the end. This engagement of yours—are your family happy about it?'

Tamara was taken aback. She wasn't used to people questioning her so frankly, and was annoyed with herself for hesitating slightly before replying coolly,

'I have no "family"—my parents are both dead, but I can assure you that there's nothing to disapprove of in Malcolm. In fact,' she added dryly, 'there are those who consider him something of a catch.'

'I wasn't talking in the material sense,' Dot explained, ignoring Tamara's withdrawal. 'I was talking about the fact that you're going to marry a man who, it seems, sees your body as something to be ashamed of rather than delighted in. I thought that attitude to sex had disappeared long ago.'

'Just because Malcolm isn't a sex maniac, it doesn't mean that we won't be happy together,' Tamara retorted stiffly.

Dot shook her head in bemusement, as though she couldn't believe what she was hearing.

'Oh, my dear,' she said sadly, 'I hope you know what you're doing. You're throwing away one of life's greatest pleasures, you know. Things were different when I met George, there wasn't the freedom there is now, but from that very first moment I knew beyond any doubt that I wanted him physically very much indeed. I did have girl friends like you, though, many of whom found out too late that without sexual desire marriage can be a very arid state indeed. Forgive me for speaking so frankly—I can see I've offended you, but you remind me very much of my own daughter . . .'

'It's perfectly all right,' Tamara told her, relenting in the face of the other woman's patent distress. 'I suppose I am being a bit touchy, but I know Malcolm and I will be happy. For one thing . . .' She hesitated and then plunged on bravely, 'Well, to be honest, Dot, I just don't think I have a particularly high sex drive. In fact . . .' She hesitated, wishing she hadn't begun the conversation, realising that for the first time in her life she was revealing things about herself she had never ever revealed before—and to a stranger.

'Don't say any more,' Dot insisted sympathetically. 'I think I know what's on your mind, Tamara, but believe me, I don't think you're right—you just haven't met the right man. When you do you'll discover a side of yourself you never dreamed existed, and he, if he's got any sense, will delight in helping you to discover your real sensuality.'

For some reason Tamara shivered, suddenly conscious that she was standing in the shop still wearing the brief bikini.

'Buy it,' Dot urged her. 'Take the first step on the road to discovering yourself.'

She wanted to refuse and had fully intended to do so, but somehow she found herself leaving the boutique half an hour later clutching a glossy black carrier with the boutique's name scrawled in gold across it, still wondering what on earth had possessed her.

George was waiting for them by the noticeboard on which the hotel pinned details of trips and activities they organised.

'This sounds interesting,' he told them, indicating a handwritten notice headed 'Rain Forest Walk.'

Tamara read the details quickly and discovered that the hotel had organised a walk through the tropical rain forest which began on the slopes of the island's volcanic mountains and which would take the better part of a full day.

'We set off from here about eleven, drive to the rain forest, and then have lunch prior to starting the walk,' George told them. 'The manager here tells me that it's well worth going. I hadn't realised it, but apparently the rain forest covers a good two-thirds of the island; because the volcanic mountains are so steep they've never been cultivated, and the forest never cleared. It extends for several hundred square miles, and the paths are only known to a handful of local guides. I'm told that we stand a good chance of seeing some rare butterflies; and the parrots, of course.'

'I don't know if I fancy it,' Dot told him frankly. 'Won't there be creepy-crawlies and snakes?'

'Apparently not—there aren't any snakes on the island.'

Tamara was tempted to put her name down for the walk. It sounded interesting, and after two days of simply lying soaking up the sun she was ready for something a little more physically demanding. As St Stephen's was comparatively undeveloped there were very few organised tours apart from those involving cruising round the island and stopping off at various secluded bays for swimming and beach parties.

'I think I'll go,' she announced impulsively. 'I rather like the idea. When is it?'

'Tomorrow,' George told her. 'How about it?' he asked Dot. 'Shall I put our names down?'

'I suppose you might as well. It will be something to tell the kids about.'

'Yes, I must remember to take my camera, they'll enjoy seeing a shot of Mum "exploring the jungle",' George teased her.

In the end all three of them added their names to the short list.

'The Somerfields—those are the young honeymooners, aren't they?' Dot asked her husband, scrutinising the list. 'The Brownes and the Chalfonts—that's the foursome who came together. They're all in the fashion business,' she explained to Tamara. 'Alex Browne is a designer, apparently. Oh,' she added, 'Zachary Fletcher's put his name down. In fact he was first on the list.'

'If he's been involved in an accident perhaps he needs the exercise,' George suggested. 'I noticed when we got off the plane with him that he was limping slightly.'

Zachary Fletcher! Tamara wished she had not decided to go. For some reason the dark-haired man disturbed her. Telling herself that it would look odd if she backed out now, she contented herself with the conviction that Zachary Fletcher was hardly likely to notice her; and then wondered why she should find the knowledge faintly depressing.

'I think I'll go up and change,' she told the Partingtons. 'I want to try and do a bit more sunbathing, especially if there won't be time tomorrow.'

'Wear your new bikini,' Dot urged her. 'We might see you later on the beach.'

When she went up to her room Tamara had no intention of changing into the cyclamen bikini, but she couldn't resist taking it out of the bag, still amazed that she had actually bought it, knowing she would never wear it, and then, governed by some impulse she could not understand, she hurried into the bathroom and quickly changed into it, before she could change her mind, and not daring to visualise Malcolm's reaction to her scantily clad body.

Picking up a white towelling robe and shrugging it on, she collected her book and the bag containing her suntan lotion and glasses before hurrying back outside.

The sun beat down with an intensity that burned right through her protective robe, and Tamara decided to forgo the beach in favour of the privacy of the gardens. She found a secluded spot protected by a low-growing hedge of tropical shrubs, their huge trumpet-shaped scarlet flowers almost too perfect to be real. The huge beach towel she had brought with her gave her something to lie on, and having smoothed as much of her body as she could reach with suntan cream she donned her glasses and picked up her book.

Half an hour slid by, before the book began to fail to hold her attention, which she found wandering to the antics of a tiny humming-bird darting in and out of the creeper adorning the walls of a nearby block of self-contained suites, and Tamara marvelled at the way the tiny creature delved so energetically in search of food.

She turned over, easing her stiff shoulders, tensing instinctively as she saw the black jean-clad legs in front of her, before her eyes moved slowly upwards over taut masculine thighs and a muscular chest before coming to rest on the saturnine face bent towards her.

Her skin went hot, burning with embarrassment as he glanced cynically over her body, so intimately revealed in her brief bikini.

'Very provocative, but wasted here,' he taunted softly. 'Why aren't you on the beach?'

Tamara suddenly found her voice, which to her chagrin was shaking with the pent-up force of her anger.

'Why should I be?' she demanded. 'If you must know, I came here because I wanted . . .'

'To be alone,' he finished mockingly. 'Snap! So what do we do now? Makes ourselves an interesting item of gossip or . . .'

Tamara scrambled to her feet, feeling at a distinct disadvantage lying at his feet like . . . like a sacrificial offering.

'If you want to be alone, Mr Fletcher,' she replied, stressing the formality of the 'Mr', 'then I suggest you find somewhere else . . .'

'I like it here,' he told her calmly. 'It's quiet and

it's private.' His teeth glinted in a white smile, the grooves either side of his mouth deepening, giving Tamara a glimpse of the man he might possibly be when he wasn't either bored or indifferent. 'Be a good girl,' he suggested. 'I'm sure you'll find plenty of young men to admire you on the beach, and attractive though you are, I'm really well past the age where I'm incited to lust by the sight of a pretty girl with very little on.'

Throughout this speech Tamara's eyes had gradually widened, as her body stiffened until she was staring at him in frozen outrage, scarcely able to speak for the anger building up inside her.

'I don't know what you're trying to imply,' she gritted out at last, hands clenched furiously at her sides, 'but if you're suggesting that I came here deliberately because you . . . because I knew you come here, you couldn't be more wrong. You see,' she told him sweetly, releasing the fingers of her left hand and raising it a little, 'I don't happen to need to run after other men—I've already managed to catch mine!'

She knew it was a vulgar little speech, but she really didn't care; she didn't care about anything but banishing from those green eyes the expression which said, quite plainly, that he thought she had deliberately come to this part of the gardens dressed as she was because she hoped to attract his attention.

'I had no idea that you came here,' she finished with a flourish. 'If I had I would have made a point of avoiding it.'

'Would you indeed?' His eyes were on her left hand, narrowed and faintly assessing. 'Are you sure about that? Girls have been known to do strange things when they've been . . . deprived of their fiancés' presence.'

'You're an expert on brief affairs with other people's girl-friends, are you, Mr Fletcher?' she asked scornfully. 'Well, you can relax—I'll never be deprived, or depraved enough to trouble you.'

'Oh, it wouldn't be any trouble,' she was assured with a smoothness which caught her off guard. 'Not normally, that is.'

His glance seemed to stroke over her heated body, drawing from her a brilliant look of hatred, and her fingers curled in on themselves again.

'It's just that I prefer to do my own hunting,' he added, further enraging her. 'Now be a good little girl and run away and play with someone else, mm?'

When Tamara eventually reached her room she gave vent to her fury, removing the garments which she was sure had caused Zachary Fletcher's preposterous insults and hurling them on to the floor. How dared he suggest . . . How dared he look at her like that . . . How dared he imply that . . .

Cheeks flushed, her eyes sparkling angrily under their fine brows, she turned on the shower, subjecting her body to a vigorous scrubbing as though by doing so she could punish it for encouraging Zachary Fletcher to believe she was the sort of girl who behaved in the way he had implied. And even if she was a man-chaser, she would never, ever in a million years, chase after someone like him, she decided through gritted teeth as she dried herself. Never!

CHAPTER TWO

IT was shortly before ten forty-five when Tamara walked into the hotel foyer to join the small group of people waiting there for the guide for the rain forest walk.

She saw Zachary Fletcher straightaway, but ignored him, deliberately going to join Dot and George Partington, who were chatting to the foursome they had mentioned the previous day.

'Are you looking forward to it?' Dot asked her, and when Tamara said that she was she added curiously, 'By the way, what happened to you last night? I looked for you at dinner time, but I couldn't see you.'

'I ate in my room. I had a headache—probably too much sun,' Tamara lied, knowing full well that the reason she hadn't dined in the restaurant was that she wanted to avoid any further contact with Zachary Fletcher. It would have been just her luck to run into him in the dining-room and for him to accuse her of deliberately arranging it that way. Not even the brief evening telephone call she received from Malcolm had soothed her, and she was still burning with a resentment which refused to fade.

'You're looking very attractive, anyway,' Dot told her, admiring the olive cotton jeans Tamara was wearing with a white tee-shirt with toning stripes in olive and rust. Over her shoulder Tamara had slung a large canvas beach bag with a slightly thicker long-sleeved sweat-shirt, sunscreen, and some other bits and pieces in it, the canvas almost exactly matching the dull olive of her jeans. The outfit had been bought especially for her holiday—Malcolm didn't care for women in jeans, and Tamara had had to buy a pair of jodhpurs especially for her visit to his parents, who kept a couple of hunters for Malcolm's and his father's use.

Malcolm had insisted on Tamara learning to ride—it was expected that she should, he had told her when she protested that she was not likely to get much opportunity to use her newly gained skill in London.

She had drawn the line at hunting, though. Much as she enjoyed the stirring sight of the huntsman with his hounds and the riders in their red coats she had no wish to emulate them.

Dot introduced her to the cheerful quartet she and George had been talking to. Alex, the fashion designer, was slim and fair-haired, his wife Sue dressed in a pair of high-fashion baggy trousers cleverly linked to the top and the man's shirt she was wearing belted with gold suede.

Their friends, Heather and Rick Chalfont, were Alex's business partners, although more on the financial side than the fashion, Rick explained.

'Don't you find it lonely being here on your own?' Sue asked her.

'Not really. I came away for a rest . . .' Dot had turned away to talk to Zachary Fletcher and Tamara was unbearably aware of his lean, sardonic face, the mocking expression in his eyes as they rested momentarily on her flushed skin.

'Yes, the build-up to a wedding can be wearing,' Heather agreed sympathetically. 'When is the big day, by the way?'

'We haven't decided finally yet. Malcolm—my fiancé—has to go to New York soon, and he isn't quite sure how long he'll need to be there. Once he gets back we'll fix a firm date.'

'Hardly an eager bridegroom, then?' Zachary Fletcher drawled, joining in the conversation. 'Haven't you warned him what happens to laggards in love?'

Despite his reference to the old Border ballad Tamara knew that he was implying that she was the one urging Malcolm into a marriage he wasn't too keen on, and she longed to be able to tell him that he was quite wrong and that Malcolm simply wasn't the type of man to rush anything.

'Oh, we all have trouble getting our men to the altar these days,' Sue laughed. 'That's what comes of sexual equality. There isn't the same need to rush that there used to be—It's much better too, don't you think?' she appealed to Tamara. 'Just imagine marrying a man and not knowing the slightest thing about him sexually. It's almost as archaic as an arranged marriage to a stranger.'

'Yes,' Tamara agreed blankly, hoping that her expression wouldn't betray her, but how could she admit in front of Zachary Fletcher that her sexual experience of any man, let alone Malcolm, was practically nil?

Oh, there had been a few tentative caresses when she was in her teens, but shyness and Aunt Lilian's stern lectures had withered any natural desire to experiment, and as the years had gone by she had grown more and more ashamed of having to admit the truth. Not even Malcolm knew that she was a virgin. The subject had never come up, and for the first time she began to wonder how Malcolm would react. There had been a time in her late teens when

she had begun to think that the truth must be
written all over her face, and it had made her
awkward and shy when she was approached by
boys, but it was something she had eventually
overcome.

It had been obvious that Zachary Fletcher hadn't
guessed the truth, and she had to fight down her
rising anger as she remembered the previous afternoon.

When Sue claimed Dot's attention to her horror
Tamara found her bête noire at her elbow, looking
hard and intensely masculine in the same black
jeans, this time with a cotton shirt, which again
had long sleeves and was unbuttoned only at the
throat, where she could just see the first crisp tangle
of body hair shadowing his chest.

'I hope you aren't going to accuse me of joining
the walk simply to force an acquaintance with you,'
she managed to say in an undertone.

'Hardly.' The creases in his face deepened as he
smiled. 'I'd have to be paranoic to do so, wouldn't
I, seeing that I put my name down first. Do you
enjoy walking?'

He didn't really sound as though he cared
whether she did or not, but Tamara forced herself
to answer politely.

'Yes, I do. I was brought up in the country . . .'

'Well, today's jaunt won't be any country stroll.
These mountains are pretty steep and I believe the
jungle is extremely dense . . .'

'Are you trying to put us off?' George joked,
suddenly joining in the conversation.

'Not at all. I probably gave the wrong impression. To tell the truth, had I thought the walk
would be too arduous I wouldn't be attempting it
myself.' Zachary Fletcher touched his left leg as he

spoke, and Tamara remembered George saying that he had seen him limping.

'I was involved in an ... accident,' he added tersely, obviously reading the question in George's eyes. 'I'm here to recuperate, and take enough gentle exercise to get myself fit to resume normal work.'

'You're in the Army, I believe?' George prodded.

'Yes.'

The word was completely devoid of expression, but Tamara had been looking at his face as he spoke, and she caught her breath as she saw it change visibly, closing and hardening, a shutter coming down over his eyes. What on earth had there been in that innocent question to provoke a reaction like that? Unless of course he had been cashiered or some such thing. She had heard of such happenings from Malcolm's father, and knew they were a terrible disgrace ... What did it matter why he had reacted the way he did? she asked herself. She couldn't care less about the man.

'Looks as if our transport has just arrived,' George commented. Outside the hotel were two Land Rovers, equipped with extra seats, and open to the fresh air.

'Everyone ready?'

Everyone was. The quartet were first at the Land Rovers, followed by the young honeymoon couple. Tamara was about to sit beside them when the guide prevented her.

'You sit in next one,' he told her. 'I sit here,' and she had perforce to join Dot and George in the rear Land Rover, her heart thumping uncomfortably when Zachary Fletcher slid his long length in beside her.

There wasn't a lot of room in the vehicle; Dot and George were both inclined to plumpness, and Tamara could feel the heat of Zachary Fletcher's thigh burning through the thin fabric of her jeans. She tried to move away surreptitiously, but it was impossible to do so without squashing up to George.

The guide climbed into the foremost Land Rover and shouted something to the driver and they were off.

The road leading from the hotel complex was smooth and well tarmacked, but the moment they turned off it they were on a road which by the looks of it had been neglected for years. As the wheels of the Land Rover plunged into a huge pothole Tamara was flung bodily against Zachary Fletcher. It was like running full tilt into a stone wall, she thought breathlessly as his arm came out to save her and she was held against the hard, muscled wall of his chest and the taut flatness of his belly. It could only have been seconds before he released her, but they were the longest seconds of Tamara's life. The heat of him seemed to burn right through her thin clothes, imprinting itself against her body. Scarlet colour ran up under her skin as she realised that just as she had been aware of the male contours of his body so he must have felt the soft fullness of her breasts.

'Tamara, are you all right?'

Dot's anxious query intruded on her thoughts. 'I'm fine,' she assured her, adding formally, 'Thank you, Mr Fletcher. I was caught off guard.'

There was something distinctly enigmatical about the look he gave her. 'It happens to us all,' she was assured, 'and please . . . call me Zach, Tamara.'

'Oh, just look at that view!' Dot exclaimed, drawing attention away from Tamara's faintly flushed cheeks. 'Have you ever been to the Caribbean before, Zach?'

'No.'

All of them looked to their right, where the ground fell away to the sea, a vivid and impossible blue melting into lilac mists on the horizon.

'It's so beautiful!' Dot sighed.

'But very poor,' George reminded her. 'I can't get over the poverty in which a lot of the islanders still live. When you're here you begin to understand the pull Communism has for some of these people.'

'You're right,' Zach agreed. 'Already there are strong left-wing groups in all the Caribbean islands. They get their education and training in Cuba, and unless the West starts sitting up and taking notice we're going to wake up one day and find we've lost the Caribbean.

'Oh, no politics, please!' Dot protested. 'Let's not spoil our holiday! Tamara, just look at that building perched down there on the hillside. It looks as though it's amost ready to fall into the sea!'

It was quite a long drive to the beginning of the rain forest, made worse by the appalling condition of the roads. Although St Stephen's was one of the largest of the Caribbean islands, it had been very badly neglected; however, the hotel manager had told Tamara that they were hoping that the revenue from tourists would help to improve the facilities of the island.

The plain which stretched from the coast to the rain forest was dotted with banana plantations, the island's main crop, and after a while the novelty of seeing the fruit protected from the insects by bright blue plastic bags began to wear off. The closer they

got to their destination the more aware Tamara
became of a certain tension in the man seated on her
left. There was nothing in the relaxed manner in
which he lounged in his seat to betray any emotion.
His face was slightly averted as though he were
studying the countryside, so that all Tamara could
see was the taut line of his jaw and the dark hair
growing low in his nape, but the aura of tension
emanating from him was unmistakable; she could
feel her own nerve endings shivering in primeval
response, and she wondered what was wrong.

'Oh, that must be the restaurant,' Dot commented when a solitary building appeared on the
edge of the plain just where the volcanic mountains
rose steeply to the sky, their sides clothed in thick
tropical vegetation.

The plain itself seemed to be completely bereft
of dwellings of any sort, although one or two dusty
cart tracks looked as though they must lead to
either villages or houses.

'Most of the plantation owners built their homes
on the Atlantic side of the island,' Zach explained
when Tamara commented on the uninhabited
landscape. 'It was considered to be healthier—and
less likely to be attacked by pirates.'

His face seemed to relax a little as he spoke to
her, the bones softening a little from their previous
fixed rigidity, and then the Land Rovers started to
climb up towards the restaurant.

Made of wood, its original green paint had long
ago faded to a dull olive, and inside, despite the
overhead fans, the air was thick and clammy.
Tamara had never felt less like food, and while the
other members of the party settled themselves at
the long trestle tables she went back outside, finding it both cooler and fresher.

'Not hungry?'

She hadn't realised that Zach Fletcher had followed her, but shook her head mutely, unwilling to admit to the momentary weakness which had overcome her inside the restaurant.

'Me neither.'

The admission surprised her and her expression betrayed the fact. 'What's the matter?' he asked grimly. 'Aren't insensitive brutes like me allowed to have normal feelings?'

'I never said . . .' Tamara began defensively, but he cut her short, and mocked, 'You never said, no. You didn't need to, those eyes of yours say it all. Quite a contradiction, aren't you? On the one hand we have the modern, liberated young woman, holidaying apart from her . . . fiancé, and yet those eyes could belong to a sheltered novice, with no more idea of modern mores than a babe in arms.'

'If you'll excuse me, I've decided that I'll have something to eat after all,' Tamara said pointedly, brushing past him, but once inside the restaurant she could do no more than drink a glass of lemonade and toy with the salad she had ordered.

It was after two o'clock when their guide preceded them along one of the paths leading from the restaurant up into the mountains.

Within half an hour Tamara was perspiring heavily, glad of her cotton tee-shirt, and she wasn't the only one. Everyone seemed to be feeling the effects of the intense humidity, even, to her surprise, Zach Fletcher, whose shirt front was dark as his perspiration soaked into it, and yet unlike the other men he made no move to either roll up the long sleeves or discard the shirt altogether. Perhaps it was because he knew how darkly attractive he looked in the black shirt and pants, Tamara thought acidly, instantly dismissing the thought as stupid; he wasn't the sort of man who needed to attract female attention by dressing dramatically; even in the same type of floral bermudas and shirts favoured by some of the more flamboyant guests, any woman worthy of the name would give him a second look.

The deeper they progressed into the forest, the more closely entwined were the trees; mahogany predominant among them; vines twining chokingly around them, dead and decaying vegetation lining the forest floor, the sweet rotting smell making Tamara long for a breath of clean, fresh air. Once or twice their guide stopped to point out to them an orchid, growing among the rampant greenery, and occasionally the laboured sound of their breathing was broken by the shrill screech of a parrot, although they never actually glimpsed the birds. On several occasions they could hear the sound of water, but they never came in sight of any of the streams which the guide told them ran through the forest, with apparently spectacular waterfalls in places.

Tamara regretted her decision to join the walk; there was something oppressive and unwholesome about the forest and its environs, something that made her flinch and long to be out in the open once more.

At her side Zach seemed to be having no problem in keeping up with the others, despite his claim that he was recuperating from an accident, but at one point when the guide called a halt and Sue shrieked out suddenly when she caught sight of a small lizard, Tamara, who had been looking in Zach's direction, saw him pale suddenly beneath his tan, perspiration beading his skin, his fingers curling into his thigh.

'Are you all right?' Her low, impulsive question seemed to free him from whatever had held him in its grip, because his face suddenly seemed to relax.

'Fine,' he assured her hardily. 'Come on, I think our guide's ready.'

They tramped through the forest for over two hours, Tamara steadily growing more and more oppressed by the entwining branches blotting out so much of the sunlight, and the heavy, unreal atmosphere around them. It was almost as though she had stepped into one of the enchanted forests of her childhood, and now, as then, fear mingled with the feeling of unreality.

They had climbed quite steeply, the path sometimes so narrow that they had to walk in single file. At one point, as promised, the rain suddenly started to fall, in saturating sheets which penetrated even the thickness of the vegetation, and the guide, who had come prepared, handed out umbrellas, large enough for two people to shelter under together.

Tamara shared hers with Zach, marvelling at the abruptness with which the rain came and went.

'It's something you get used to,' Zach told her laconically, causing her to comment in surprise, 'You said you hadn't been to the Caribbean before.'

'I haven't, but one jungle's very much like another.'

He didn't say anything more and Tamara had the conviction that subject was not one he wished to take any further. For some reason they seemed to have been teamed together for the walk—possibly because everyone else was already with somebody, and she wished passionately that she had never decided to participate in the walk. She didn't like the atmosphere pervading the forest and she didn't like the prickles of awareness she experienced every time some inadvertent movement brought her into physical contact with Zach Fletcher.

He glanced at his watch and frowned.

'We ought to be heading back. There's no dusk as we know it at home here. Another couple of hours and it will be fully dark.'

He walked forward, catching hold of the guide's arm, and spoke to him. The guide shook his head vehemently.

'No turn back yet,' he told Zach. 'Soon, but not yet. Not much further now,' he added with the air of a commander urging his flagging troops to greater effort.

'How much further can "not much" be?' Sue groaned when they had walked for another fifteen minutes. 'I'm bushed!'

Tamara could only agree. She felt hot and sticky and was longing for a cooling shower. Perspiration had darkened the front of her hair, and her mouth felt dry. She was also beginning to regret the lunch she had refused, distinct pangs of hunger assailing her. She had some biscuits in her bag, but it was too much effort to put it down and search for them. Everyone else seemed tired too; everyone, that was, apart from Zach, who despite the sweat stains marring his shirt, still seemed able to keep up with their guide without flagging.

Ahead of her Tamara saw the guide stop. They had reached a small clearing where a fallen tree had created a tiny space.

With groans of relief the small party came to a standstill, with the exception of the guide, who for some reason appeared to be slightly nervous.

Tamara watched him as his eyes darted round the clearing as though looking for something. Zach wandered over to her side.

'Something wrong?'

He too was watching the guide, and although he hid it well Tamara thought she glimpsed a certain disquiet in his eyes, before he veiled them and said smoothly, 'Ready for the return journey? I——'

He broke off suddenly as the clearing was invaded by half a dozen men carrying machine guns and dressed in camouflage fatigues.

At her side Tamara heard Zach swear under his breath, and then they were being herded together like so many cattle, the muzzle of one gun pressing icily against Tamara's throat as she stumbled over an exposed tree root.

'Just what the hell is all this about?' Zach addressed the question to the man who was obviously in charge of the small group, and it seemed the most natural thing in the world for him to take command; none of the other men challenged his right to do so, and Tamara suspected they were all, like her, too dazed, to think of asking the question 'why'.

Motioning to them to keep still with his gun, the man came forward while two of his men menaced them with raised guns.

'You are to be held hostage until our Government releases the men it wrongly imprisoned six months ago,' they were told in excellent English. 'It is time the rest of the world knew what is happening here in the Caribbean. We are tired of incompetent Capitalism, governments who allow us to starve, who refuse to educate children above the age of fourteen, who condemn their own people to a life of poverty and degradation.'

'Holding us hostage would not alter anything,' Zach told him. 'But if you release us without harm now, I promise you that we will make sure that you are allowed to put your view to your Government.'

None of them moved a muscle. They were all looking to Zach to provide a lead they could follow. Tamara couldn't believe it was actually happening. She looked round for their guide, but he was nowhere to be seen. Dot was clutching George's arm, her face pale and strained. The two honeymooners were in each other's arms, while Sue and Heather moved a little closer to their husbands. Only she had no one to turn to.

'Yes, and then they would throw us in prison with our comrades,' the guerrilla sneered. 'No, my friend, we need you too much to release you. Without you our Government will never set our comrades free; they will be shot. Come...' he ordered roughly, 'we have four hours' march ahead of us. It will be at least that time before your hotel raises the alert, and by then they will have no chance of finding you. Very few people know this forest as well as Kennedy here does,' he told them, with a jerk of his gun in the direction of a grim-faced islander, one of the two who was standing over them with a gun.

Out of the corner of her eye Tamara saw Heather sway towards Chris, her face paper-white.

'Oh, God help us, Chris,' she moaned softly. 'What are we going to do?'

Her words seemed to release a wave of panic over all of them. Tamara herself shivered uncontrollably despite the clammy heat; only Zach remaining cool and controlled in the face of their predicament.

'Come,' the leader of the guerrillas commanded. 'It is time to leave.'

'You can't get away with this!' Alex Browne protested in a tight voice. 'The English Government . . .'

'Is many thousands of miles away, my friend,' the guerrilla mocked him, 'and the time when nations were prepared to risk any confrontation for the sake of their subjects is long past. Your Government will do nothing for you . . .'

'And neither will yours for you!' George burst out. His skin had an unhealthy purplish tinge and Tamara saw Dot reach out towards him, shaking her head warningly.

'It's his blood pressure,' she murmured to Tamara, adding in terror, 'Oh, my God, what's going to happen to us?'

'You cannot expect us to walk as fast as your men,' Zach pointed out to the guerrilla. 'If you intend to take us all hostage you will have to keep us alive—your Government will never hand over your comrades in return for lifeless bodies, and if you want to keep us alive you will have to make allowances . . .'

The islander frowned, appearing to consider Zach's statement, and then turned and said something in a rapid patois to one of his companions, who shrugged and grimaced.

'We cannot afford to waste time,' he told Zach.

'And neither can you afford to take risks with our lives,' Zach replied smoothly. 'Wouldn't it be simpler to just take one of us hostage, while allowing the rest to go free? Especially if we were to guarantee that your story was printed in the British newspapers; that way your cause would receive far greater publicity than it would simply by holding us to ransom. Your own Government is hardly likely to make public the knowledge that people cannot holiday safely on St Stephen's.'

Tamara held her breath while the guerrilla leader consulted with his companions. Would he accept Zach's suggestion? She had no doubt that if he did, Zach intended to be the one to volunteer to remain behind, and she wondered if she had been mistaken after all, and he was in some way connected with the Army. It wasn't a question she could ask.

The sun was dropping swiftly towards the horizon, fear an almost tangible emotion in the small clearing as they waited for the guerrillas' decision.

'You,' their leader commanded roughly, turning back to Zach, 'do you give your word that what we want will receive publicity?'

'Whoever said that the pen is mightier than the sword knew what life was all about,' Zach muttered sardonically under his breath to Tamara, as he inclined his head, and then looked across at George.

'Mr Partington will inform the British Consul of what has happened and of our bargain—the freedom of my companions in return for publicising your cause.'

'Our Government has no wish to quarrel with Britain and is sure to release our comrades once it is known that we hold a British hostage.'

Tamara wasn't so sure. There had been several cases in the Press recently where lone Britons had been kidnapped and held for many months without the Government doing anything to negotiate their freedom. Or at least that was the way it seemed on the surface.

'Very well then,' the guerrilla leader pronounced. 'Your companions may go free.' He shouted a command to one of his men, who came forward, machine gun at the ready, and indicated that they were to follow him.

Tamara went last, unable to resist one backward glance at Zach. He was standing with his back to them. What was he thinking? she wondered. Was he afraid? Surely he must be.

'Wait!'

The curt command halted her, as the guerrilla leader stepped forward and grasped her arm. She had been walking alone at the rear of the small column and she shivered under the cold assessment of eyes that seemed to strip her clothes from her body.

'You will stay.' Turning to Zach, he added grimly, 'Alone you might just be foolish enough to try to escape—you have the look of that sort of man about you, my friend, but now that we have your woman you will stay. And if you try to leave we will kill her.'

From a distance Tamara heard Dot's brief protest, before George silenced her, unaware of the look of helpless appeal in her eyes as they clung to Zach's rigid back.

It seemed an aeon before he turned, pivoting round slowly, no expression at all in his eyes.

'Do not argue with me,' the guerrilla leader told him, 'otherwise they shall all stay.'

'You're wrong,' Tamara wanted to protest. 'I'm not his woman,' but the words stuck in her throat. She couldn't bear to look at the others as they stumbled out of the clearing, her last hope that the guerrillas might relent and allow her to leave fading as she heard their footsteps die away.

'Come,' the guerrilla leader ordered. 'It is time we left. You were right,' he told Zach, 'the others would have held us up. If you try to delay us by falling deliberately behind I shall give your woman to my men. It is many weeks since they have had a woman. Our camp is remote, and our life there too spartan to attract women like yours.'

Tamara, who had gone ice-cold when she heard his threat, refused to look at Zach, too mortified by the guerrilla's assumption to meet his eyes. Why didn't he tell the other man the truth? That they were little more than strangers.

She knew the answer several seconds later, when, under the pretext of helping her up a steep incline, Zach muttered softly to her, 'I know what you're thinking. This isn't the time for petty conventions. If I told them the truth I'd be condemning you to gang-rape. As long as they think you're my woman they won't touch you. Even among mercenaries there's a certain code of ethics, and besides, they probably think that if any of them tried to touch you I'd react in the same way that they would in similar circumstances—kill with my bare hands,' he elucidated grimly, 'and none of them would want to be the one I took with me before they cut me in half with those neat little Russian toys they're carrying!'

CHAPTER THREE

DARKNESS fell with the swiftness of a cloak, enveloping the forest in a heavy blackness that threatened to stifle Tamara. Its only mercy was that it obliterated the sight of the men guarding them, their guns never moving a fraction from their threatening positions.

With the fall of night came the rain; not rain such as she was used to at home, but an actual curtain of water which started without warning, and ceased fifteen minutes later, leaving them with their clothes plastered to their backs, and the track beneath their feet slimy with thick mud.

Tamara lost count of the number of times she stumbled; she had long ago lost track of time. At first she had tried to keep her spirits up by telling herself that soon the others would be back at the hotel; the alarm would be raised and they would be rescued, but she knew she was living in a fantasy world. It would take the others at least four hours to get back to the hotel, by which time they could be anywhere. The jungle seemed to press down upon her, tautening her nerves until she was ready to scream and run, heedless of what might happen.

As though he sensed how close she was to losing control, Zach grasped her arm. An hour or so before she would have bitterly resented the familiarity, but now she was helplessly grateful for it and its reminder that she was not completely alone.

'Faster!'

The gun was cold against her flesh and she shuddered, almost losing her footing as she tried to hurry. At her side Zach increased his pace, the grip of his fingers biting into her arm, and she remembered that he was recovering from an accident and that George had told her that he limped slightly. The pace the guerrillas were setting was gruelling; Tamara ached in every muscle, even a simple activity like breathing was excruciatingly painful, but at her side Zach seemed to be completely unaffected—he wasn't even breathing faster—unlike her.

She stumbled again as the path started to rise, sprawling almost full length, despite Zach's attempts to save her. Above her she heard the unkind laughter of their captors, and weak tears flooded her eyes.

'Get up!'

It was Zach speaking, his voice iron-hard and inflexible, cutting through her self-pity.

'I can't go any further,' she protested wearily.

'Oh yes, you can,' he replied grimly, 'and will—unless you want to be left here to die. These guys aren't playing games, and they don't make allowances. Now get up. I value my life even if you don't value yours.'

He had spoken so quietly that Tamara had had difficulty in hearing him, his voice deliberately flattened to prevent the words from carrying, and once again she remembered his profession.

'It's all right for you,' she protested bitterly. 'I suppose you're used to this. You . . .' Her breath was cut off savagely as she was hauled to her feet and held against him, while his mouth came down on hers, almost depriving her of breath. Again she heard the men laughing, but this time in a different way.

It was only seconds before Zach released her from what hadn't been a kiss at all really, more a harsh punishment, her lips bruised from the abrasive pressure of his, her nostrils full of the musky male scent of him. Just before he stepped away from her, he gritted furiously, 'You little fool! Any more cracks like that and we'll both be dead, understand?'

Too late, she did, all too well, and as she walked on on shaky legs, couldn't stop herself from visualising what might have happened had any of the guerrillas guessed what she was going to say. The information that Zach was connected with the British Army, in no matter how nebulous a fashion, was bound to provoke an unpleasant reaction.

Half blinded by tears, sick and shaking, Tamara forced herself to go on, not knowing who she hated the most, Zachary Fletcher or the guerrillas.

How long they walked along that narrow winding track which she felt sure must be circling the mountains instead of climbing them Tamara didn't know; she only knew that the physical effort of simply putting one foot in front of the other was a greater ordeal than anything she had experienced in her life; there was no room for thought, or even fear, only the sheer physical necessity of keeping going.

The sporadic downpours of rain were something she had become accustomed to, like the soaking clothes plastered to her skin and the discomfort of walking in wet shoes. As they brushed past trees and through dense undergrowth, so thick in places that it almost obscured the trail, Tamara felt as though she had strayed into a horrendous nightmare of the sort where, during her childhood, she had been forced into headlong flight, pursued through the gnarled and tangled blackness of a forest by some nameless but terrifying oppressor.

A damp tangle of leaves brushed her skin and she felt a momentary sharp pain, but her brain was too weary, too involved in the process of simply walking, to register more than faint surprise. It was only later when yet another of the huge moths which seemed to infest the forest flew in front of her face and Tamara raised her arm that she realised what had happened, her whole body stiffening in primeval fear and horror so that Zach, who had been walking behind her, cannoned straight into her.

His 'What's the matter?' turned into a small sound of understanding as his fingers circled her wrist with hard warmth and found the alien body of the huge leech which had attached itself to Tamara's soft flesh.

Her scream was suppressed instinctively, her eyes closing in childish reaction to blot out the sight of the pulsing body of the leech as it clung to her arm.

'Move!'

This time Zach ignored the harsh command, forcing the guerrilla leader to drop back to see why they had stopped.

'Your flesh is tender and more to their liking than ours,' he commented when he saw what had happened. 'Here.' He tossed Zach a box of matches and asked laconically, 'Do you know what to do?'

'I think so.' Calmly Zach struck one of the

matches and applied the flame to the body of the leech. Tamara watched in dazed horror as the bloodsucker shrivelled and dropped to the ground. Her body was trembling so much she could barely stand, shock waves of reaction flooding over her, drowning out everything but her revulsion for what had just happened.

'Walk!'

The gun thrust into her side reminded her of her surroundings, and obediently she started to move slowly along the trail. They must have come miles. What time was it? She wasn't wearing a watch and found it impossible to calculate the length of time that had passed since their capture.

The higher they climbed the less dense the vegetation became; although it was still thick enough to provide a thick screen to cover the steep slope they were ascending. Tamara could remember reading in her holiday brochure that because of the climate even the tops of the mountains were covered in heavy foliage, and the more time went on the more she came to realise the implausibility of them being rescued quickly.

At last the guerrilla leader called a halt, although Tamara could see nothing in their surroundings to distinguish it from anywhere else on their trek.

'That way,' he instructed, motioning them towards a sheer-sided mass of shiny black rock. 'Hurry!'

It was only when they drew nearer that Tamara realised that what she had mistaken for a narrow cleft in the volcanic rock face was, in actual fact, the entrance to a much deeper fissure.

'I discovered this place when I was a boy,' the guerrilla leader told them, adding boastfully, 'I doubt there are half a dozen people on St Stephen's who know of its existence, and certainly no one who would be able to lead anyone here.'

Tamara could well believe him. She shrank back instinctively from the almost Stygian darkness that seemed to reach out greedily for her as they approached the fissure, and this time it was Zachary Fletcher who urged her on, his face unreadable and remote, as though his thoughts were elsewhere.

The fissure was so narrow that they could only walk through it in single file, and Tamara, who had always had a horror of being underground, felt her skin crawling with a terror remembered from a childhood visit to the caves at Inglewhite, many years before. But this time there were no understanding parents to hurry her out to the welcome fresh air, and she bit down so hard on her lower lip to prevent herself from protesting that she could taste the blood.

At last, when she felt she could not stand another second trapped in that narrow passage, it opened out into what was obviously a series of caves. The first one was empty, and despite the number of openings leading off from it, the guerrillas seemed to have no difficulty in selecting one of them, and herding their prisoners into it.

This time the tunnel was mercifully short and it opened into a large cavern, well lit by Calor gas lamps which threw eerily reflected shadows over the shiny rock face. Furniture of the type used on camping holidays—folding canvas chairs, a table, a cooker next to a container of gas with a fridge on the other side of it—was scattered incongruously inside the cavern, and as though he sensed her surprise, the guerrilla leader laughed at Tamara.

'Even men such as we need our "home comforts", but do not be deceived, we are quite capable of living off the jungle if need be.

'Kennedy,' he addressed one of the men over his shoulder, 'make us some food, while I show our guests to their quarters. You will be very comfortable,' he threw over his shoulder to Tamara. 'I shall give you the honeymoon suite.'

The raucous laughter which followed the gibe made Tamara shudder with nausea.

This time the passage they were taken down was wide and comparatively short. It ended in a cave furnished in a way that made it obvious that careful planning had gone into their capture. For one thing there was a heavy wooden door set into a frame built into the rock face; a heavy bolt on the outside of the door.

'Even if by some miracle you should manage to escape and get as far as the main cavern, it will avail you nothing. I have given my men orders that you are to be shot if you try to leave—not killed, you understand, but wounded in such a way as to make you . . .'

'Crippled for life,' Zach supplied curtly.

The vulpine grin which acknowledged his words brought a fresh wave of sickness to Tamara. Her eyes slid feverishly over the cave, noting first the sleeping bags on the floor and then the primitive sanitary arrangements, and she willed herself not to betray her feelings to either of the two men watching her.

'Everything for your comfort,' their jailer mocked. 'Until we have word that our comrades are to be released you will be locked in this room at all times.'

'But what will we do, what . . .'

'Oh, I'm sure you'll find some way of passing

the time.' The leer which accompanied the words made Tamara feel almost faint with fresh revulsion.

She stood with her back to the door until she heard it close and Zach move softly behind her, tension tightening her shoulders.

'What's going to happen to us?'

She hated herself for asking the question; for sounding like a helpless emotional woman, and her fingers curled protestingly into her palms as though to deny the impression created by her words.

'For the moment—nothing. I'm sorry you had to be involved in this.'

'It wasn't your fault. At least you managed to persuade them to free the others.'

'We have to talk,' said Zach.

'About what?'

'About how we're going to get out of here,' he said calmly. 'There's no point in placing any reliance on them freeing us. The days are gone when governments gave in to the threats of groups like the Red Brigade.'

Tamara felt faint. 'You mean . . .'

'I mean God helps those who help themselves,' he told her curtly. 'Our only chance is to escape.'

As though he was aware of the effect of his brutal disclosure he came towards her, placing his hands on her shoulders and swinging her round to face him.

'I'm not saying this just for the sheer hell of it. We have to face facts. We've been taken hostage by a small-time group of terrorists who probably know as well as we do that their Government won't free their comrades, but that the death of two innocent holidaymakers will get them worldwide newspaper coverage.'

'But you've already promised them that,' Tamara protested, not wanting to believe him.

'They want to make an impact; surely you're familiar with the scenario by now? They aren't the first group to try something like this, and they won't be the last.'

'No. There was that African coup last month. I read about it in the papers. The S.A.S. went in, didn't they?'

'Two dozen of them,' Zach agreed harshly, 'to rescue two men; twenty-six in all, but only eighteen got out alive . . .'

'I didn't read that.' She frowned. Zach's face was almost grey in the harsh lamplight, etched with bitterness and a weary cynicism she had come to recognise.

'You wouldn't,' he told her grimly. 'We don't publicise our failures—it's bad for morale.'

We! Her heart thudded to a standstill, her eyes mirroring her disbelief.

'Oh yes, it's quite true. I'm not hallucinating. I was there. I was the one responsible for losing eight lives.' He swore viciously under his breath, and then added contemptuously, 'Oh, on paper it wasn't my fault. There was no way we could have known about the bomb. But they were my men. They followed me, and I led them to their death.'

'And your accident?' Tamara's throat ached with pity, her mouth dry as she was caught up in his tension.

'You want to see what the debris from a bomb does to the human body, do you?' he demanded savagely, ripping open the buttons of his shirt and removing it in a violent motion. 'Then take a good look!'

Somehow she managed not to betray her shock

at the sight of the scars still livid and raw against the taut tanned surface of his skin.

'So that's why you always wear a shirt.' She swallowed, unable to stop her eyes moving downwards, and as though he read her mind he said softly, 'You want more?'

'Stop it! Stop tormenting yourself!'

'Myself? I thought you were the one I was tormenting, or aren't you going to admit that the sight of my body made you feel sick? Of course it doesn't affect all women that way. There are some—those who are sick themselves, who actually enjoy looking at this sort of thing.' He grimaced bitterly. 'When I left Africa I told myself there was no way I was ever going back to the jungle. The gods must be laughing at me right now.'

Tamara remembered how tense he had been earlier on and her heart was touched with pity.

Sounds outside the door made her stiffen and glance uncertainly towards him. The next instant she was in his arms, the fierce heat of his body pressed against hers, his hands sliding beneath the wet fabric of her tee-shirt, one holding her helplessly against him, while the other covered the soft swell of her breast.

Her protest was silenced by the pressure of his mouth, his eyes hard and warning as the door swung open behind her. The angle of his body forced her off balance so that she had to grasp his shoulders to prevent herself from falling backwards.

To an onlooker they must look passionately oblivious to anything but themselves, she thought hazily, her senses reeling under the impact of so much alien masculinity. When Malcolm kissed her it was with suitable restraint, and he certainly never held her against him in a way that made her intensely aware of every bone and muscle beneath the taut covering of his skin. Time was suspended as wave after wave of emotion crashed down over her, swamping her with the knowledge that here at last was a man who could stir her senses and bring her body to tingling, aching life. It was like a revelation, but so brief that by the time Zach released her, Tamara had almost persuaded herself that she had imagined it.

'We want to keep them as off guard as possible,' he explained when their guard had gone. 'That way we stand a better chance of escaping.'

'We can't escape,' Tamara whispered, turning away from the bowls of stew the man had placed on the floor.

'We have to. It's either that or die. What have you got in there?' he asked, indicating her canvas bag, which she had dropped on the floor.

'Nothing much. Just a few things I carried with me on the plane. No machine gun . . .'

Her weak attempt at a joke didn't generate any response. Zach was already down on his hands and knees reaching for her bag.

Tamara took it from him.

'One sweatshirt—now damp,' she enumerated, 'a pack of wet wipes—a girl I work with recommended them for long-distance travel. She's flown all over the world.' There wasn't much else in the holdall—a few articles of make-up, a small towel, two packets of biscuits and some small change.

'The first thing we ought to do is to get out of our wet clothes,' Zach told her unemotionally. 'Oh, come on,' he added impatiently, when he saw her expression. 'We're both adults, and I'm not saying it out of some prurient and infantile desire to see your body. We're in the tropics, and although we've both had our shots I doubt we have the immunity to fever and disease that our friends out there possess, and I for one don't fancy falling ill up here without recourse to a doctor or even the most basic curative medicine. Neither do I want a sick person on my hands, so if you won't undress yourself you'd better believe that I'll do it for you. After all,' he added sardonically, 'it won't be the first time you've undressed in front of a man, will it? Or does your fiancé normally do it for you?'

He caught her hand as she raised it, bruising her wrist with the pressure of his grip, mockery gleaming in the depths of narrowed green eyes as they surveyed her flushed and angry face.

'Very convincing, but hardly necessary. Your morals aren't any concern of mine. Now are you going to stop acting like an outraged virgin and strip off or am I to do it for you?'

'I'll do it myself.'

'Somehow I thought you would,' he mocked as his hands went to the belt of his jeans. Tamara swung round immediately, glad of the opportunity to hide her burning cheeks. It was silly to feel so selfconscious, she told herself. After all, her underclothes were no more revealing than the bikini he had already seen her in, and yet there was something about the enforced intimacy of their surroundings that made her fingers tremble over their familiar tasks.

'With any luck these should be dry by morning.'

The combination of level tones and matter-of-factness made it possible for Tamara to follow Zach's example and spread her wet jeans out on the floor of the cave, but she couldn't bring herself to look at him, fiddling with the contents of her canvas holdall until she was sure he had moved away. She stood up and almost collided with him, the shock of his unexpected proximity driving the breath from her body.

'Now what's the matter? And don't try telling me you've never seen a man before. Is it this?'

'This' was the puckered scar disfiguring his thigh. Tamara shook her head, unable to trust her voice, shocked by the visual impact of his powerfully muscled body, so alienly male; primitive and powerful, the black briefs which were his sole covering doing little to disguise his masculinity.

'If you want to use the—er—facilities,' he gestured to the chemical toilet in the corner of the room, 'I'll turn my back.'

It was the final indignity. Tears blurred her vision. She had never felt more degraded or despondent. She longed for the shower in her hotel bedroom, for any means of feeling really clean and fresh so long as privacy came with it.

'No?' His eyes surveyed her clinically in her brief lacy bra and tiny matching pants. 'Better not let any of our friends see you dressed like that,' he drawled, his expression changing suddenly, something approaching excitement glittering in his eyes as he breathed, 'Yes . . . perhaps that's it.'

'Perhaps that's what?' Tamara demanded crossly.

'Nothing. Let's try and get some sleep. Tomorrow threatens to be one hell of a long day.'

After the initial comfort of the fleece-lined sleeping bag, the cave floor began to seem hard.

To her left Tamara could hear the even rise and fall of Zach's breathing; he apparently had no difficulty in finding the escape from their situation which persisted in eluding her.

At last exhaustion overcame the fear-induced adrenalin which kept her mind feverishly alert and she fell asleep, but even then there was no escape. Nightmare succeeded nightmare and she muttered protests in her sleep, tossing restlessly within the narrow confines of the sleeping bag.

In one nightmare they were walking through the forest again, and once more she felt the needle-sharp pain as the flaccid body of the leech attached itself to her skin. Her cry of terror was strangled beneath the heavy weight oppressing her; the years rolled back and she was a child again, turning to the comfort of a small bedside light to find solace from her fear of the dark; waking from a frightening dream with her father's name on her lips and feeling the comforting protection of his arms banishing the bad dream.

Tamara awoke to darkness, pleasantly warm and comfortable, the aftermath of sleep dulling her senses. At first, confused by the heavy warmth of the body resting close to her own, the arm curving her body close against it, she thought stupidly that she must be with Malcolm, his name a perplexed whisper on her lips, because when had Malcolm ever held her like this? When had she ever felt this weak desire to seek the protection of his embrace with an intensity that went deeper than mere instinct?

The arm holding her stiffened, a dark, tousled head lifting and materialising out of the darkness as a cool voice drawled, 'Sorry, but you've got the wrong man. Do you often make mistakes like that?'

Zachary Fletcher! Tamara bit her lip, closing her eyes in helpless dismay.

'I thought you were my fiancé,' she said dully,

unaware of the way his eyes hardened in the darkness, narrowing on the soft thrust of her breasts half exposed by her restless movements.

'Sorry to disappoint you, but I've no intention of standing in for him,' he mocked her, withdrawing his arm and leaving her suddenly bereft. 'You were restless during the night. You cried out in your sleep, but it wasn't for Malcolm.'

What was he implying? That she had cried out another man's name—another lover? How could that be?

'I must be going soft,' he added jeeringly, 'and I bet I'm not the only man who's heard you call "Daddy!" in that lonely hurt little voice. Pity you haven't got a razor in that bag of yours.' He had completely changed the subject before she had time to respond to his earlier taunt, the clever change of topic leaving her fuming but unable to defend herself.

He glanced swiftly at the heavy, masculine watch strapped to a hair-roughened wrist. 'Seven. I wonder if they intend to feed us this morning. Oh, they won't let us starve,' he assured her as the flare from the lamp he had just lit illuminated her face. 'There wouldn't be any point. They've obviously gone to some trouble equipping this place. I wonder how often they need to get supplies. They can't store much up here—not when everything has to be carried up manually. We'll have to try to catch them off guard, that way we can observe their routine. No, don't put that on,' he commanded, removing the sweat-shirt from Tamara's fingers as she was on the point of reaching for it.

Again her face betrayed her, and he laughed shortly. 'Don't worry, I'm not going to rape you—it isn't my scene.'

She heard sounds outside the door and the sound of the bolts being drawn back, but the agonised glance she cast Zach was ignored, so that the man entering with the tray had a clear view of her breasts covered only by the flimsy cups of her bra, the naked lust in his eyes making her blood run cold with horror, her eyes pleading mutely with Zach for protection as she remembered the warning the guerrilla leader had given them when he first announced that Tamara was to remain captive.

To her astonishment Zach didn't repulse her, although it was several days before she realised why. The bulk of his body came between her and the guerrilla, shielding her from the hot, burning desire she had seen in his eyes, his arms so protective as they closed round her that this time she didn't protest when his lips came down on hers in a briefly provocative kiss. However, she hadn't been prepared for the hard warmth of brown fingers cupping her breast, nor for the throbbing response of her flesh as her nipples hardened in answering awareness, her whole body trembling with the onset of an emotion she refused to comprehend.

'Good,' Zach exclaimed with very evident satisfaction as the door closed behind their jailer. 'That, I think, will reinforce their belief that we're lovers, and remind our friend of all that he's missing.'

'What do you mean?' Tamara could still remember the fear that had filled her when the guerrilla looked at her; not because of any physical attributes she might have possessed which attracted him, but because it had been the look of a predatory male animal for the means of slaking his lust and she had recognised as much on a deeply instinctive fear.

Mercifully, or so she thought later, he didn't tell her—then.

The day passed as others were to pass; some of it spent in the close confines of their cave and the rest in the main cavern with their jailers, who gambled for small change, smoked and drank while listening to the radio they had brought with them, presumably for some mention of their kidnap.

When they had been imprisoned for three days Tamara began to lose hope that they would ever be free. Zach had made no further mention of escaping and she had come to the conclusion that he had thought better of it after considering the odds against them.

She ought to have known better.

On the fourth night of their incarceration, just as she was about to crawl into her sleeping bag, Zach said abruptly, 'Don't go to sleep yet. I want to talk to you.'

CHAPTER FOUR

HUNCHING her arms round her raised knees, Tamara stared at him. The beginnings of a beard shadowed his jaw. He had managed to persuade one of the guerrillas to furnish him with a razor, although he was never allowed to remove it from their presence, but by dusk each day the dark regrowth stubbled his skin, tonight as always prickling Tamara with the awareness of the intimacies she shared with him.

'Tomorrow some of the men are going down to the main town to collect fresh supplies—I overheard them talking. The patois they use is very similar to French Creole and I was able to understand most of what they were saying. Only two men will be left behind to guard us. Tomorrow we have to escape, Tamara,' he told her with heavy emphasis on the word 'have'. 'It may well be our only chance.'

'But how can we?' she protested. 'There may only be two men, but they'll both be armed. We don't even know our way out of the caves!'

'I know the way,' Zach assured her tersely, 'and as for the guards. . . . You do want to escape, don't you?'

'Yes.'

'Very well then, listen. Tomorrow when the guard brings our breakfast I want you to distract him long enough for me to get his gun.'

'Distract?' Her forehead creased in a bewildered frown.

'Oh, come on, or do you want me to spell it out for you? You're not some unknowing little virgin, Tamara. There's only one sure-fire way of successfully distracting him long enough for me to take him by surprise. You don't have to let him touch you, if that's what you're worried about,' he added harshly. 'The way he's been looking at you for the last four days, just a simple come-on from those huge grey eyes should be enough to do the trick. Especially if it's accompanied by a little bit of sexual enticement.'

'No! You can't expect me to do something like that!' Distaste mingled with fear, leaving an unpleasant taste in her mouth and a heart thudding with shock.

'It's the only way,' Zach told her curtly. 'And if we have to stay here much longer I can't see him keeping his hands off you in any case. You heard what their leader said. It's been weeks since they've been anywhere near a woman, and you can't have missed the way he's been looking at you.'

'You said none of them would touch me,' Tamara reminded him thickly.

'I'd forgotten what sort of effect abstinence can have on men like them,' came the dry retort. 'Living the way they do strips away the veneer of civilisation.'

'I can't do it!'

'You must. Pretend it's your precious fiancé if it helps.'

Long after Zach had fallen asleep Tamara lay awake staring into the darkness, fingernails digging into the palms of her hands. She had seen the way the men looked at her, and especially the one detailed to bring them their food, and had been revolted by the way his eyes had roamed hotly, and increasingly boldly, over her body. Was Zach right? If they stayed here . . . Her mind shied away from the implications of what he had said. Wasn't it enough that she had already had to endure all manner of physical degradation, forced to share this cell with him, was she now to be forced into actively encouraging the mental rape of her body?

Despite her conviction that she would never fall asleep, the next thing Tamara was aware of was Zach shaking her. Disorientated for a few seconds, she lay on her back, staring up at him, transfixed by the green eyes that seemed to watch her with an almost hypnotic intensity. Wasn't that how animals of prey stalked their victims, she thought wildly, by using the power of their eyes to dull their sense of self-preservation?

'I can't do it, Zach,' she told him huskily.

'You can, and you will.'

The calm words brooked no opposition, but neither were they bullying or forceful. They were more like the calm reassurances of a parent to a child uncertain of its ability to perform a difficult task.

A few seconds later, while she was deliberating between wearing her sweat-shirt or the button-up tee-shirt she had worn when making the walk through the forest, Zach handed her the shirt.

'Wear that,' he told her softly, 'and help me to roll up our sleeping bags. They'll come in useful if we do manage to make our escape. I don't know how long it will take us to reach safety, but it certainly won't be accomplished in one day.' He looked up. As usual he seemed to have heard their breakfast approaching far sooner than Tamara, and she tried to quell the trembling building up inside her as the footsteps drew nearer.

'How do you know the other men have left?' she whispered, feeling her courage desert her.

'They intended to leave at first light. They never bring our breakfast until well after that.' He looked at her for a moment as they heard the man fumbling with the lock, and then before Tamara could stop him he wrenched open the neck of her blouse, exposing the creamy curves of her breast, ignoring her sharp, terrified protest.

'You're acting a part,' he hissed at her. 'You're Eve personified; you've seen it done a thousand times, and you're playing for the most precious prize of them all—your life!'

As the door opened he turned away and she was left alone to face the leering look of their jailer as he entered with the breakfast tray, his eyes sliding hotly over her exposed flesh, the tiny flames leaping to life there making her go rigid with terror.

For a moment she thought she was going to faint, and then with an almost superhuman effort she forced her lips to part in a stiff parody of an enticing smile, her hand going clumsily to the man's arm.

His response was immediate, the sourness of his breath overwhelming her as he grasped her by the waist, the bearded face thrusting closer to her own.

'You want a real man, do you? Well, you have found one in Jaimi,' he boasted, his hot breath grazing Tamara's forehead, a calloused hand sweeping upwards towards her breast, as she closed her eyes in mortal terror and disgust, her stomach heaving as her entire body clenched inwardly against the assault to her flesh. As the guerrilla swung her round, obviously intending to carry her to her bed, Tamara had a momentary glimpse of Zach's face; unfamiliar in its hard-boned cruelty,

his eyes glittering like frozen jade in a face suddenly
devoid of all colour, and then there was a brief
movement, the fiery dance of light along the blade
of the knife he had removed from the guerrilla's
sheath, a sudden hissed gasp and the suffocating,
relentless weight of the man's body as it fell across
hers, crushing her to the ground, until Zach pushed
it aside and lifted her to her feet, mouthing words
she could not hear because her mind was full of
the silent screams of her body and the man who
had just died because of his desire for it.

'Tamara!'

There was a brief, stinging pain, her cheek on
fire where Zach had struck her, and the screams
faded, to be replaced by the calm decisiveness of
his voice.

'We have to hurry. Roll up your sleeping bag—
that's right. And the food. We have to hurry. Give
me your holdall, and the sleeping bag, you can
carry the other one. No, don't look at him.' He
walked softly to the door, and returned, the man's
machine-gun slung over his shoulder in a casual
manner which did nothing to deceive Tamara. For
the first time she was seeing him in his natural
habitat without any camouflage; she was seeing
him as the predator with the killer instinct that he
really was. She knew beyond any shadow of a
doubt that the gun was merely window-dressing.
She had seen the way he had killed the guerrilla—
without a sound, with the greatest economy of
movement—and a shudder went right through her.

'Quietly,' he cautioned her as he urged her out
into the corridor. 'Now, just follow me, understood?'

He must have a photographic memory, she
decided, as he led her unerringly into the main

cavern, which to her relief was empty. Tamara had no idea by which route they had reached the cavern on their initial journey, but Zach seemed to be in no doubt at all.

They were within three yards of it, having carefully skirted the perimeter of the huge cavern when Tamara's heart practically stopped still to see the figure emerging into the cave.

Zach moved so fast he was little more than a blur. The man didn't even see him to anticipate the blow that felled him to the ground, his body lying so awkwardly that Tamara knew instinctively that he was dead.

'There's no point in leaving him alive to come after us,' Zach told her as they reached the tunnel. 'With any luck the others won't be back for at least a day—possibly two, and by that time we should have gone far enough for them not to be able to pick up our trail. I daren't risk the path they used to bring us up here—there's too many of them for that.'

'But how will we find our way back?' Tamara protested. 'We've no maps, no compass. The guerrilla leader said that the forest paths are known only to a handful of men.'

'True, but there are other ways. There's the sun; and the stars. Finding our way back is the least of our problems. The most important is preventing them from finding us.'

When they finally emerged into the daylight Tamara was almost blinded by it, and she stood blinking, delighting in the warmth of the sun against her skin, weak tears of relief suddenly filling her eyes. Every step of the way out of the cave she had expected to be confronted by their jailers, and that, added to her terror of the enclosed space, had robbed her of the last of her self-control. Tears poured unchecked down her cheeks as she stood, trembling, unable to move.

'Tamara!' She heard the impatience in Zach's voice and looked mutely at him, hearing his muttered curse, but not aware of anything until she felt the warmth of his arms round her, his breath grazing her temple, the muscles of his thighs taut as a bowstring as he let her lie against him.

She lifted her head, wanting to tell him that she was all right, but looking into the jade depths of his eyes was like drowning in icy green seas. Motivated by a force she could barely understand, she raised trembling fingers, impelled to touch the hard bones of his face, surprised to find how warm his flesh felt to her touch, her breathing oddly constricted, strange sensations coursing through her body, her heart beating almost suffocatingly fast. Bemused and dazed, her lips parted in involuntary invitation, her eyes watching the downward descent of his head, the hard gleam in his eyes, as ruthless as any hunter intent upon its prey.

The touch of his lips against hers was shatteringly cataclysmic, reaction exploding inside her as his mouth moved questingly over hers, destroying everything but the feeling beating up inside her. And then suddenly Zach's face disappeared and in its place was the face of the guerrilla, and pleasure turned to nausea, the blood draining out of her face as she shuddered in revulsion.

'What the . . .'

'That man. The way he touched me . . . the way he looked at me . . .' The whispered words held the echo of her horror, her eyes darkening at the remembered degradation.

'It's over,' Zach told her crisply. 'Forget it.'

'How can I?' Tamara demanded wildly, almost on the point of hysteria. 'Every time a man takes me in his arms I'm going to remember . . . to be revolted . . .'

'That's enough! You're behaving like a girl who's never experienced any physical intimacies before. You're an engaged woman . . .'

'And because of that I'm not allowed to have any feelings, any . . .'

'We'll talk about it later,' Zach told her, grasping her arm and hurrying her away from the small clearing. 'Right now I want to put as much distance between the caves and us as I possibly can. What are you worrying about? That your fiancé might disapprove? I'm sure when you tell him it was either that or losing your life, he'll understand, and nothing happened, after all.'

Perhaps it hadn't in the sense that he meant, but apart from his kisses it had been her first sexual experience and it had left her feeling defiled in a way that no amount of logic could wipe away.

If Tamara had thought she had been driven to the limits of her endurance on the long trek up to the caves, it was nothing to the gruelling pace set by Zach once they had escaped from their guards.

A machete he had taken from the cave helped him to force a path for them through the dense undergrowth of the forest, and Tamara, following in his wake, could only marvel at the decisiveness with which he seemed to know instinctively which path to take when several converged, although it wasn't until late in the afternoon that she learned how he had known and what he had been looking for.

Every muscle in her body throbbed in protest at the strain being placed upon it, but she daren't ask for a respite in case her body stiffened up so much that she couldn't get going again. The path had grown steadily muddier, but plodding doggedly in Zach's footsteps it was several minutes before she realised that the dull, muted roar she could hear was running water.

'That's what I've been looking for!' Zach exclaimed in triumph when they eventually came in sight of the spate of water cascading over rocks to bubble frenetically down miniature rapids.

'We can follow it—with luck, all the way down to the coast,' he explained to Tamara. 'I knew there must be streams running through the forest.'

'But how did you know how to find one?' Tamara asked breathlessly, trying not to wince as her aching legs protested mutely.

'The state of the ground; animal tracks heading to what I hoped would be water. Simple knowledge known to any Boy Scout.'

But although he minimised his skill Tamara could not. Without his training they would never have escaped, never found this stream, and yet even while she acknowledged these facts she felt a faint frisson of fear prickling across her skin. There was something about Zach, something alien and untamed, something so overwhelmingly male that at times she wanted to run from him and keep on running.

'Tamara?'

She hadn't realised he was watching her.

'I'm all right,' she lied listlessly. Her period of captivity had not prepared her for what almost amounted to a forced march through rough jungle terrain.

'We'll stop soon,' Zach promised her. 'Fortunately the stream isn't very deep here, although it's flowing too fast for us to take any chances. We'll walk through it as far as we can. If they do track us as far as the stream it might help to put them off the scent.'

Following Zach's example Tamara removed her trainers, knotting the laces and slinging them round her shoulders.

'You might as well take off your jeans as well,' Zach told her laconically. 'It will save them getting soaked.'

With shaking fingers she did as he suggested, telling herself that the embarrassment she felt was stupid in view of the intimacy they had shared while they were captive. But then it had been different, she argued mentally, something alien quivering to life within her as Zach studied the vulnerable length of her legs in the tiny briefs which were no more revealing than the bottom half of a bikini, and yet somehow ... Was it her imagination, or had the jade eyes darkened slightly as he looked at her?

Although she didn't realise it, something of her feelings was mirrored in her eyes, causing Zach to say dryly,

'Relax—I might be a crude, uncouth soldier, but I promise you I don't share my fellow professionals' lust for your body. The degenerative effect of civilisation! Disappointed?'

'I'm engaged to another man, remember?' Tamara retorted, her chin firming and lifting. 'And besides,' she let her mouth curl fastidiously, 'men who indulge in physical violence have never appealed to me.'

'Meaning that my scars revolt you? Try remembering that they were gained trying to free innocent but important civilians. I'm no mer-

cenary, Tamara; no would-be hero trying to prove
something to the world. As far as I'm concerned
it's simply a career.'

'Killing people!' Tamara lashed out stormily.
'Don't you realise that if it weren't for men like
you, there wouldn't be these terrorists?'

His eyebrows rose as he turned in mid-stream to
stare at her. 'You think not? It's the age-old story,
Tamara, which came first, the chicken or the egg.
You can't use sweet reason on men controlling
guns like these and trained to use them.'

'Aren't you ever afraid?' Tamara whispered,
shivering suddenly despite the steamy heat of the
forest, chilled by some unknown, primitive fear
that was purely feminine.

'Afraid?' At first she thought he was deriding
her, and then she saw the expression in his eyes.
'Of course I'm bloody well afraid,' he told her.
'Every time I go out on a mission; and every time I
come back. When you go out you've got the adrenalin working for you, but coming back.' He turned
away, his face withdrawn, Tamara forgotten as he
said slowly, 'Coming back is going through hell.
You've made it—this time, but you've always left
someone behind; someone so close to you that
they're a piece of your own body, each time you
die a little, and this time . . . You asked me if I'm
ever afraid.' His lips twisted with self-derision. 'I
was shot as we were escaping. If it hadn't been for
two of my men I'd be lying dead in the African
jungle with the others. They tell me that while I
was in hospital I pleaded with them never to send
me back to the jungle. That's how unafraid I was.'

Tamara couldn't speak for the lump in her
throat, overwhelmed by an urge to go to him and
comfort him as though he were a small child, which

was ridiculous when she looked at the lean open masculinity of him.

'That's one of the reasons I came out here,' he told her. 'I wanted to prove to myself that I could face the jungle—and win.'

'And you have,' Tamara said quietly.

'We're not out yet,' he advised her. 'Are you worried now that you know the truth?'

'No,' she said honestly. In her own mind there was no doubt that the circumstances Zach had told her about so unemotionally had resulted from the death of his men rather than any fear for his own safety. She was also a little surprised that he had chosen to confide in her—surprised and, more worrying, flattered.

It was dusk before Zach decided that they could stop. They had travelled several miles downstream, forced out of the water when the currents grew too swift for Tamara.

'We'll sleep here,' Zach told her, indicating a spot farther away from the stream than she had anticipated.

'So that the sound of the water doesn't drown out the sound of anyone's approach,' he explained patiently to her. 'We can't risk lighting a fire, but we won't need one. How do you feel about avocados and bananas for dinner?' he asked her, nodding towards trees bearing both fruits, adding, 'At least that's one thing we don't have to worry about!'

Tamara enjoyed the fruit, but longed for a drink of water. Zach, however, refused to let her touch any. 'I know it looks clean, but that doesn't mean it is. You have no immunity to whatever might be in it, and I can't afford the added handicap of having you ill.'

Forced to acknowledge the logic of this, she

asked Zach if she could at least wash in the stream before going to sleep. Water to wash in had been scarce in the cave, and because of Zach's proximity and her own inherent modesty she had made do with sketchy ablutions during their incarceration. Now, however, after the sticky heat of their march she longed to feel coolly cleansing water against her skin. They were camped not far away from a deep natural basin which had filled with water to form an oval pool, and ever since she had set eyes on it Tamara had been imagining the luxury of immersing every inch of her body in it. But Zach soon dashed these plans.

'Go ahead,' he told her easily. 'I'll come with you.' He didn't seem to share any of Tamara's selfconsciousness, simply stripping off his shirt, his back to her, revealing the solidly packed muscle, sheathed in raw silk flesh whose only imperfections were the scars still puckering it where they had yet to heal.

His hands were on his belt buckle when he turned, a subtle sensuality in the look he turned on Tamara.

'What's the matter?' he taunted throatily. 'Never seen a man undress before?'

The faintly derisive curl of his mouth told her that he thought he knew the answer, and a deep shudder racked her as she forced herself to turn away, knowing that the scarlet colour burning in her cheeks was a sure-fire giveaway. Not until she heard the clean splash of his body hitting the water did she turn, reluctantly abandoning her earlier intention of bathing nude in the still clear water and settling instead for paddling about cagily in the shallows in her bra and briefs, reluctant to risk the deeper water—and Zach.

Without waiting for him to emerge from the water she clambered over the stones worn smooth by the constant action of the pounding water and hurried back to the small clearing where they had left their belongings. She was struggling to ease her still damp body into her sleeping bag when Zach returned, grim-faced, his shirt knotted round his waist, his lips clamped tightly together.

'Just what the hell do you think you're playing at?' he demanded without preamble. 'This isn't some children's outing we're on. From now on we stick together, do you understand that?'

'All I did was come straight back here,' Tamara flashed back. 'I'm not one of your men, you know. I don't have to obey your orders!'

'That's right,' he agreed with a pleasantness which immediately alerted her to the very unpleasant gleam in his eyes. 'You don't have to, but if you want to stay alive you'd be much wiser if you did. What would you have done, for instance, if you'd got back here and found our friends waiting for you?'

Her face gave her away, even though she struggled to suppress her memories of the morning.

'Exactly so,' Zach drawled, letting her know that he knew exactly what was going through her mind. 'So from now on, you don't make a move without me knowing about it, understood?'

She hated him, Tamara thought resentfully as she tried to make herself comfortable in the narrow sleeping bag. The earth felt hard beneath her, Zach was breathing easily beside her. Before he climbed into his own sleeping bag Tamara had watched him moving quietly about the clearing. Setting up early warning alarm systems, he had told her grimly, adding that if they were to make steady progress every day they would need to sleep properly at night and the precautions he was taking meant that if anyone approached their camp, the sound of their approach would wake him in time to be ready for their arrival.

'Simple survival tactics,' he told her when she marvelled.

Contrary to her expectations she fell asleep almost immediately, worn out by the physical exertion of the day, but it wasn't a restful sleep, being punctuated by tormenting images dominated by the lascivious grin on the face of the guerrilla as he reached for her body.

'No!' The word was wrenched from her lips, bringing her sharply awake to find herself pinioned by steel fingers, the heavy weight of a man's body pinning her to the ground. Reason was obliterated by primeval panic; the weight of the man above her that of the guerrilla, the scream bubbling in her throat cut off sharply by the hand clamped across her mouth.

'Tamara!'

The crisp sound brought back reality, and the tension drained out of her body as swiftly as it had seized it.

She shuddered convulsively, her voice husky with emotion. 'I'm sorry—I was having a nightmare. That man ...' She shuddered again, taken off guard when Zach sat up abruptly, taking her with him so that her head was pillowed against his shoulder, moonlight revealing her expression to him.

'It bothered you as much as that?'

Her face told him the answer, the way she cringed away from him as he lifted his hand to push the heavy swathe of hair out of her eyes causing him to stop and look at her, and then very slowly and deliberately raise his hand to her face, drawing his knuckles gently across her skin before stroking lightly downwards along her throat, and over her shoulder.

Her breath seemed to be trapped in her throat. Her whole body had gone tense, her eyes those of a hunted animal crouched to flee. His fingers touched her breast and she arched away from him, her whole body jerking as though she were a puppet, the colour draining out of her face, leaving it white and anguished before she started trembling with a sickness that stemmed from her memories of the morning; the guerrilla reaching for her, touching her, Zach stabbing him and then the blood ... She moaned deep in her throat, the trapped, hunted cry of someone in mortal terror.

'Tamara, it will be all right. You'll forget ... when you're back home with your fiancé.'

'No!' Her shudder of revulsion was unmistakable. She couldn't bear Malcolm to touch her. She couldn't bear anyone to touch her.

'Strange ...' Zach was almost talking to himself, 'I could understand your reaction if you were inexperienced, unaware sexually, but you're not. You're a very desirable young woman in her twenties, and presumably your fiancé hasn't been your only lover, unless you've been engaged since you left school. As I've learned recently, it's best to face our devils and exorcise them before they grow too powerful.'

His fingers captured her jaw, tilting her head upwards, his eyes almost hypnotising her as he bent his head, his tongue exploring the soft shape of her mouth, the hard grip of his fingers preventing her from escaping.

Her initial feeling of terror and revulsion filled her with a panic that swept away her normal self-control, her head moving frantically from side to side as she tried desperately to escape the delicate probing of the warm male lips bent on teaching her pleasure instead of fear.

Zach's fingers tangling in her hair forced her head backwards his body following hers down on to the sleeping bag as she toppled over, her gasp of surprise giving Zach an unfair advantage as his mouth closed swiftly over hers, probing the soft inner sweetness, sending emotions spiralling through her that made her feel faint with bewilderment and shock.

One powerful arm kept her clamped to the moist warmth of Zach's body. He had pulled on his jeans after his swim, but nothing else, and the hand she raised to push him away came into disturbing contact with the smooth flesh of his shoulders, the crisply dark hairs tangling across his chest, abrasive against her soft palms as her hand slid away.

'You can touch me, you know,' Zach murmured silkily against her mouth as his free hand captured her nerveless fingers and replaced them against the taut muscle of his diaphragm.

'Forget what happened this morning,' he told her softly. 'Forget everything but this.'

'This' was lean fingers sliding aside the constricting presence of her lacy bra to cup and then stroke the rounded curve of her breasts, his tongue again tracing the parted softness of her lips as his thumb moved sensuously over the hardening peaks of her breasts, unleashing inside her a torrent of emotion she was powerless to control; a pleasurable pain which began somewhere in the pit of her stomach and spread slowly upwards until her body was on fire, with the need to know a more intimate possession.

As though he were unaware of the intensity of her need, Zach began a leisurely exploration of her skin, teasing light kisses against her closed eyelids where her eyelashes fluttered frantically at the tormenting caress, his hands continuing their lazy enticement of her body.

Tamara was beyond conscious thought, beyond anything but the feeling surging through her, the instinct which urged her to caress the satin smoothness of Zach's skin as she traced the hard bones of his shoulders, first with her fingers, and then with her lips, trembling in their eagerness to taste the male warmth of him. The faintly musky odour of his body excited her with its male alienness, her whole body trembling with the desire possessing her. Her body arched mutely, pleading for more intimate contact than the briefly tantalising caresses Zach was stroking upon it, pride, restraint, self-control forgotten, swept aside in the fierce onslaught of passion as she saw the jade gleam of Zach's eyes as he looked slowly along the naked length of her body and then lowered his head, trailing fire against flesh so sensitised to his touch that tiny electric shocks seemed to tingle arousingly through her.

The touch of his mouth on hers triggered off a shuddering treacherous response, alerting warning bells deep within her brain, reminding her of the danger she was courting. But she didn't want to listen; she wanted the sensual pleasure of Zach's sexual magnetism to go on and on.

'Aren't you forgetting something?'

Tamara's head snapped forward, her eyes opening as the curt words jerked her out of her trance.

'Your fiancé,' Zach reminded her dryly. 'For a moment there you almost had me fooled, but you responded far too passionately to be anywhere near as frightened as you pretended. And I don't act as substitute for any man.'

'You couldn't even begin to fill Malcolm's shoes,' Tamara lied wildly, shrinking away from him, horrified by the wantonness of her behaviour and struggling to hide the pale shape of her body from the merciless decimation of eyes without a single trace of compassion or desire.

What on earth had possessed her? She had behaved like a . . . like a . . . Like a woman in love! The thought slid into her mind with all the silky treachery of a serpent into Eden, driving the breath out of her body as she looked helplessly into Zach's impassive eyes. She loved him? How could she? She'd only known him a handful of days. It wasn't possible. It wasn't long enough . . .

Long enough to know that he possessed a hard courage she had never known in any other man, a resoluteness and dedication to purpose that almost frightened her. Long enough to know some of his most intimate fears and thoughts, so why not long enough to love him?

CHAPTER FIVE

DAWN broke in its habitual vivid splendour, and Tamara, who had been awake already for what seemed like hours, watched the slow ascent of the sun. Next to her Zach lay sleeping. During the night he had pushed free of the sleeping bag and she could see the relaxed splay of his muscles beneath the scarred and torn flesh, and her heart started to thud slowly and heavily as she relived those moments in his arms the previous evening and the truth she had been forced to face long after Zach had fallen asleep. She loved him. It should have seemed wildly improbable and hopelessly unbelievable, but as though her body had known the truth long before her mind accepted it, after the initial shock there had been an inevitability in the acknowledgement which made it impossible for her to hide any longer behind the conventional approach to 'love', namely that it was something that grew slowly and gradually, and that only infatuation was instantaneous.

In many ways Zach was everything Tamara disliked in men; he was almost aggressively sexual—something she hated, and yet how could she deny now that she had responded almost immediately to it, perhaps an indication that some deep inner core of her had known instinctively the danger he represented.

She moved restlessly in her sleeping bag, tormented by the longing to stretch out her hand and touch the hollow planes of his face; to trace its male shape and feel the rough shadowing of the dark beard beginning along his jaw.

The temptation was almost irresistible; Zach's proximity tantalised and disturbed her, and the old habits imbued by Aunt Lilian mocked her folly in allowing herself to fall so completely under his spell. He was an astoundingly sexually attractive man and couldn't have reached the age of thirty odd without becoming aware of it. In addition, his career, his close companionship with danger, honed his maleness to the point where it became a subtle challenge and one that Tamara estimated few women would be able to resist.

Why on earth should he single her out from among the dozens of more beautiful women who must have wanted him?

If it wasn't for the proximity forced upon them by their present circumstances Tamara doubted that he would have ever spared her a second glance. Aunt Lilian had often stressed during her teens that she was no great beauty. Zach moved in his sleep and the movement revealed the length of his spine down to his narrow waist. She held her breath, almost literally trembling with the desire to trace the line of his backbone, to press her lips to the scar tissue torn by some merciless assailant.

On a sudden impulse she unzipped her sleeping bag and crawled out, only one thought in her mind, and that to remove herself from temptation. She would swim in the pool, she decided—that ought to cool her down and dampen those tormenting fantasies luring her on like a siren song.

The surface of the pond was marred only by the ripples caused by the cascade of water frothing over a high fall of rocks and down into the natural basin. Tamara paused by the water's edge, and then, acting on some driving instinct that would not be denied, with shaking fingers she unclipped and removed her brief bra and panties, firmly ignoring an inner voice, very reminiscent of Aunt Lilian, which exclaimed in frigid disapproval against what she was doing.

Before she could give in to second thoughts she stepped into the water, marvelling at the silky warmth of it against her naked skin.

Aunt Lilian and the repressions she had learned from her were forgotten as Tamara gave herself up to the pleasure of the clean water against her bare flesh; a touch so gentle that it could almost be that of a lover. Blushing a little at the wayward thoughts pulsing through her, she turned over to float luxuriously on her back, closing her eyes against the intense glare of the sun, feelings which she had suppressed instinctively all through her growing years, breaking the bonds of prudery and fear as instilled by her aunt to make her aware for the first time in her life of the sensuality of her own body, so perfectly formed by nature to give— and receive—pleasure.

'Tamara!'

The word sliced through the peaceful seclusion of her surroundings, shattering her feeling of well-being. She turned over, striking out for the shore, but it was too late; she had a brief impression of a lean, tanned blue-jeaned figure standing by the edge of the pool, and then the figure jack-knifed in a perfect dive, swimming powerfully towards her, droplets of water glistening on the satin-brown skin as she watched bewitched and entranced until she realised that Zach's expression was that of an extremely angry man, something which was borne out by the way he grasped her wrist, jerking her against him while he trod water.

'What the hell do you think you're playing at?' he grated in a voice made roughly husky by the physical exercise. 'What was the last thing I said to you yesterday?'

Too late Tamara remembered him warning her not to go anywhere alone.

'It was quite safe,' she defended. 'I wanted to swim ... I couldn't last night because you were there.'

'So this morning you risk being discovered by our guerrilla friends instead? What is it with you?' he demanded savagely. 'Are you deliberately goading me, or just plain stupid?'

It was too late to explain that he had misunderstood her. Her body was betrayingly conscious of the proximity of his, her soft skin rubbed by the soaking denim clinging to powerfully muscled thighs.

'Neither,' she retorted, suddenly conscious of her own nudity and the menace which could have lurked unseen in the forest. 'I just wanted to swim—alone.'

At another time his swearing would have made her blush, but she ignored it, desperately trying to control the quivering of her body, a combination of shock and desire, rendering her almost completely helpless, dependent on the firm grip of the brown fingers round her wrists for support.

'Well, now you've had it,' Zach told her crisply, 'and it's time we made a start. We can't afford to waste any time.' As though he sensed her reluctance to follow him, he frowned, studying her downbent head, her fair hair trailing on the water like a mediaeval Venus.

'Something wrong?' he enquired dulcetly, but Tamara wasn't fooled. He was a man of iron clothed in tempered steel, and nothing less than a laser beam could penetrate that tough outer casing.

'You go on and I'll follow you,' she stammered. 'I left my clothes on the rocks . . .'

'You don't say!' He was openly mocking her now, his lambent green gaze appraising the shadowy white form beneath the water.

'Let's get one thing straight.' The mockery was despatched to be replaced with curt contempt. 'I don't care what teasing games you play with your fiancé, just don't try them out with me. I've already told you, I'm no green boy driven to insatiable lust by the sight of a woman's body. Tease me, Tamara, and you may very well find you get more than you bargained for!'

'I wasn't teasing!' Anger overcame caution, her grey eyes almost violet with the force of her pent-up emotions, small fists beating uselessly at his hard chest. How dared he imply that she had deliberately tried to tease him?

'If you knew as much as you claim to know about women,' she continued disdainfully, seeing the disbelieving look in his eyes, 'you'd know that I'm not the teasing sort.'

To her chagrin he laughed. 'Honey, you're all that sort,' he claimed arrogantly. 'But I'm not going to waste time arguing with you.'

Before she could stop him, he was lifting her from the protection of the pool, carrying her in his arms as he strode in the direction of the poolside, the water covering them both to their shoulder blades, forcing Tamara to cling on to his neck, locking her fingers behind it in the thick darkness of his hair.

He didn't stop until they reached the clearing where they had spent the night, where she was dumped unceremoniously on her sleeping bag, humiliatingly conscious of her naked body, completely revealed to his impassive gaze. The water dripped from his jeans, forming little puddles at his feet, the damp fabric pulling tautly over the powerfully masculine body.

Her mouth dry, Tamara dragged her eyes away, overcome by the same sensation of weakness she had experienced the previous evening. She supposed that it was a measure of Zach's concern for her safety that he had plunged into the pool almost fully clad, but remembering his expression when he reached her, she was forced to the conclusion that anger and not compassion had motivated the impulsive action.

She stood up, reaching for her spare top. She could wear it when she went to retrieve the rest of her clothes. Behind her she heard Zach curse and the sound of a zip sliding downwards. When she turned he had removed the soaking jeans and was standing beside his sleeping bag clad only in a pair of black briefs. Tamara touched dry lips with the tip of her tongue, telling herself that she had seen men wearing just as little on the beach, but it didn't help, and no amount of willpower seemed to be able to stop the tremors shivering through her.

'Tamara!'

She seemed to have a genius for making Zach say her name in that particular tone.

'What's the matter? Don't you feel well?' He was standing next to her, cool fingers touching her skin, his brows drawn together in a frown as he fired a volley of questions at her.

'Your skin feels hot, but not enough for a fever.

Have you had stomach-ache? Been sick?' His fingers had left her forehead to probe the soft swell of her stomach.

'I'm fine, thank you.'

Was that husky voice really her own? She attempted to push him away, but she was still trembling far too much.

'I'm fine, thank you,' he mimicked, suddenly almost savage. 'You're the epitome of the cool, in-control lady, aren't you? Apart from that brief slip last night. Will you tell him about that, your estimable fiancé? I am right in describing him as estimable, aren't I, Tamara?

'Let me see . . .' His fingers captured hers, studying her diamond ring. 'He's something in the City; very correct and proper; ambitious in his way, and you'll make him the perfect wife. Perhaps you hadn't better tell him. It might mar your perfection.'

'He'll understand,' Tamara lied shakily.

'What?' Zach demanded softly. 'That the veneer of civilisation isn't always as thick as we would like, and that you came perilously close to the point of proving just how thin it can be?'

'I didn't.' Tamara was desperate to deny the truth; not because of Malcolm, but because she couldn't bear the thought of Zach discovering how she felt about him.

'No?'

In the sudden quiet of the clearing, the word was dangerously loaded.

'No,' Tamara reiterated firmly, avoiding her eyes.

'Liar!'

She hadn't been aware of Zach moving, but all at once he was so close to her that she could see the individual pores on his skin; could breathe in the male scent of him, and her nerve ends quivered in response to his effect upon her.

'Don't touch me—I hate it!' It was the panic-stricken cry of a child, but it seemed to ignite a fire within Zach which scorched along Tamara's nervous system as she was lowered to the ground, the weight of Zach's body pinning her there, his potent maleness dizzying her senses as his mouth punished hers in a brutally forceful kiss which left her lips swollen and quivering and frighteningly vulnerable to the tantalising stroke of his tongue over the flesh he had so recently savaged.

But the desire was still there. Tamara could see it smouldering in the depths of his eyes; she could feel it in the hard tension of his body; in the hands which swept her from throat to thigh, destroying for ever her innocence and leaving her dry-mouthed and aching with a need that was wholly adult.

'Still hate me touching you?'

His eyes seemed almost black, without a single trace of compassion or remorse.

'Yes.'

Pride forced the lie, her face averting as she closed her eyes.

The sudden touch of Zach's mouth, moving moistly over the tender vulnerability of her throat, forced them wide open again, but it was plain that her defiance had driven him beyond reason. Despite her incoherent pleas he refused to let her go, pinioning her arms instead, so that she was powerless to help herself, her whole body torn by deep shudders, by his tongue's delicately tormenting tracery of first one nipple and then the other.

The sight of his dark head against her breasts

awoke in Tamara an almost primitive yearning to
know what it would be like to hold his son against
her body, but even this was banished as the expertly
questing lips moved downwards exploring the
softly trembling swell of her stomach, his fingers
stroking seductively along her thighs.

'You want me, Tamara.'

It was an assertion she could no longer deny.
Her fingers twisted convulsively in the thick blackness of his hair. His body emanated the same dry
heat as her lips, the small satisfied sounds he made
as hesitantly, and then with increasing confidence
her lips and fingers explored the male contours of
his body, encouraging her to touch and taste with
a sensuality she had never in her wildest dreams
imagined herself possessing. The tentative touch of
her tongue against the sensitive maleness of his
throat brought a response that made the heat beat
up under her own skin, her fingers digging into the
solid muscle of his chest shadowed by the dark hair
that arrowed down past his navel.

'Tamara, I want you.' The hoarsely groaned plea
was an echo of her own desire, the pulsating heat
of the thighs pinning her to the ground arousing
inside her a deeply exciting hunger which seemed
to grow with every brush of his fingers against her
skin. The passionate demand of his kisses obliterated caution and fear; her whole body trembling
with the need to know his complete possession as
she arched pleadingly beneath him, mutely inviting
the culmination of their mutual desire.

Beads of sweat dewed his forehead and throat,
tasting salty on Tamara's tongue as she touched it
delicately to his moist flesh. With a groan Zach
cupped her breast, teasing it tantalisingly for a
second before possessing the urgently aroused

peak with lips that seemed to burn where they touched.

There was a brief moment when Tamara thought he was going to leave her, and she clutched desperately at the smoothly muscled shoulders, only to realise with a thrill of increased desire that he had merely been removing the final barrier between them. His knee parted the soft flesh of her thighs, the tautly masculine shape of him at first shockingly alien, but then his mouth slid moistly over hers and Tamara forgot her prickling apprehension in the waves of melting sweetness that started to engulf her.

There was a moment when she could have drawn back, but it was swiftly gone, only Zach's surprised, and passion-drugged, 'Why so tense?—relax,' intruding upon the dream world she was now inhabiting.

Pain, swift and unexpected, lanced through her. Above her she saw Zach's face, alien and almost savage with anger, and then the moment was gone and she was soaring higher and higher on the wings of pleasure; far beyond the cobalt blue of the heavens to a place where all the colours of the rainbow exploded and dazzled all around her, before floating her back down to earth on mother-of-pearl clouds.

'Why didn't you tell me you were a virgin? Does your fiancé know what a rare prize I've stolen from him?'

The brutal words shattered her dreams and Tamara stared at him in growing bitterness, as she realised that his anger sprang from the fact that he had taken her to be a woman of experience, and simply did not want the involvement that might come from someone who was sexually unawakened.

'No, he doesn't know,' Tamara told him scornfully. 'And he won't know that I was—from me.'

Without a word Zach left her, returning several minutes later with the underclothes she had left by the pool, his flesh damp as though he had taken the opportunity to bathe—washing away her touch, Tamara thought sickly as he dropped her bra and briefs on the ground beside her and then started to pull on his jeans.

They walked in silence through the jungle, until Tamara thought she must scream with the tension of it. If only he would say something, even if it was only that she wasn't to read anything into what had happened. She knew that already, just as she knew that had they not been alone together, fighting for survival, she would never have known Zach's fiercely demanding possession.

As the day wore on the tension between them increased until Tamara's nerves were stretched to breaking point. She couldn't bear another night alone with Zach, and that and that alone kept her going when exhaustion and anguish would have overwhelmed her. She was too dazed to realise that the terrain was gradually changing, the steep slopes giving way to more undulating ground, the forest lusher, aware only of the sickness growing in the pit of her stomach, the burning shame of having given herself to a man who, for all that she loved him, thought of her only as an unwanted encumbrance. Even her fears that they might be pursued retreated as she relived those emotional seconds in the aftermath of Zach's possession when he had demanded harshly to know if Malcolm had known of her virginity; as though his prime concern was for what Malcolm might have to say when he discovered the truth, and since she knew beyond any shadow of a doubt that Zach couldn't possibly be afraid of another man's reaction she could only come to the conclusion that his anger had sprung from the fact that had Malcolm known of her virginity he might with good reason demand an end to their engagement, and she might try to turn to Zach himself for consolation.

Her face burned at the injustice of it. She would die rather than ask Zachary Fletcher for so much as the time of day. She brushed impatiently at the tickly sensation on her arm, and then froze, her scream disturbing a flock of parrots who rose screeching into the air.

Zach swung round grimly, demanding, 'What the . . .!' his expression changing when he saw the scarlet swelling on her arm.

'What was it?' he demanded briskly, reaching her and grasping her arm around the bite.

'A spider.' Tamara shuddered. 'It was huge!' For some reason Zach's face kept receding and fading, a strange lethargy affecting her ability to respond to the questions he was rapping out.

'All right, just keep still.'

She saw the glint of light on the knife he had taken from the guerrilla, but mercifully the poison the spider's bite had injected had numbed her senses, and she watched like a sleepwalker as Zach drew the blade swiftly across the swollen skin and then bent his head to suck fiercely on the cut, spitting out the blood.

'We'll rest now,' he told her tersely.

'I can go on,' Tamara lied doggedly.

'Perhaps you can, but if you do every breath you take will circulate the poison deeper into your body. You have to rest.'

Tamara opened her mouth to argue and closed

it again slowly as a peculiar feeling of light-headedness dizzied her. She was dimly aware of Zachary unzipping her sleeping bag and putting her in it, of him touching her arm, which now felt faintly numb, but it was as though it were all happening to her while she stood apart and looked on, divorcing herself from her body.

It was only later that Tamara was told the full story of their return journey to civilisation—Zach had long since gone and the nurses watching over her in the island hospital thought it very romantic how she had come to be there and delighted in telling her over and over how Zach had walked into a small village at the edge of the rain forest carrying her in his arms, her skin dry and tight with the fever which had come from the poison injected by the spider, but she had no personal recollection of the events leading up to their eventual arrival at the island's main town, transported there in a donkey cart.

The first person Tamara had seen when she eventually threw off the fever had been Dot Partington. The Partingtons had deliberately extended their holiday to be with her when she recovered, and she had been more touched by their kindness than anything else in her life.

It had been Dot who had told her, avoiding her eyes, that Zach had left the island. Malcolm had not been told of what had happened—Dot had not known where to get in touch with him, and Tamara suppressed the guilty knowledge that once she returned home she would have to face him and terminate their engagement, for both their sakes. She could no longer contemplate the sterile sort of marriage they would have and she knew she could not in all fairness marry him feeling the way she

did about Zach. Not that she was foolish enough
to believe there was any future for her with Zach.
His absence and silence only confirmed her own
thoughts which were that he wanted her to know
beyond any shadow of a doubt that whatever had
been between them had been as a result of proximity and circumstance and was now very definitely
over.

Three days after she had first come out from her
fever, Tamara was beginning to grow bored with
her hospital bed.

Dot had promised to come and spend the afternoon with her, and at the end of the week they
would all fly home.

'You're a very lucky young woman,' the doctor
told her chidingly, when he came to see her.
'You've cheated death not once but twice.'

Although the hospital authorities had had to be
told how Tamara had come to be poisoned, the
authorities on the island had deliberately shrouded
the kidnapping in secrecy—something which would
have gone against Zach and Tamara if they had
not managed to escape, Dot had informed her.

'I honestly never thought I'd see you alive again,'
she told Tamara for the umpteenth time when she
came to visit her. 'When we had to leave you
behind with those men . . . I'm sorry,' she apologised, 'I shouldn't remind you of it. It must have
been a dreadful experience.'

'Yes,' Tamara agreed listlessly, unable to tell Dot
that her memories of St Stephen's would be
among the most treasured of her life.

'Never mind,' Dot comforted. 'You'll soon be
back home with your fiancé . . .' She darted
Tamara a shrewd look. 'It's just as well you're
safely engaged, otherwise I don't see how you could

have failed to fall in love with Zach. I think I would have done myself, George or no George!'

Tamara managed a hollow laugh, diverting Dot's attention away from her betrayingly pale face to ask her what time she and George would be collecting her from the hospital. She knew she ought to be looking forward to going home, but she wasn't. All she could feel was an enervating apathy. An aftermath of the poison, so the doctor told her, but Tamara knew differently. It was nature's way of cushioning her against the agony of losing Zach. She smiled mirthlessly. Nature was fighting a losing battle. Nothing would ever make her forget; he was burned into her mind, imprinted against her flesh, a part of her until the end of her life.

CHAPTER SIX

IT was raining as the huge jet circled Heathrow. They descended through thin grey cloud merging drearily with the tarmac, the only spots of colour coming from the planes themselves with their distinctive markings.

Terminal Three was busy; there had been talk of a go-slow on the part of some of the airport's personnel, and those who were able were rushing to get away before it started, precipitating the crisis they had hoped to avoid.

Tamara said her goodbyes to the Partingtons in the restaurant, where they had insisted on taking her for a final cup of coffee.

'Promise you'll write and let us know how you're getting on,' Dot urged her, 'and any time you feel like a break you know you'll always be welcome— you and your fiancé. Did you let him know what time you were arriving back? I should have thought he would have met you, knowing how ill you've been.' There was a trace of disapproval in her voice, and Tamara hastened to defend Malcolm, explaining that she hadn't wanted to worry him and so had simply sent a cable telling him that she was extending her holiday by a week. She intended to phone him once she got home.

She said her final goodbyes to the Partingtons at the taxi stand, promising to let them know how she was getting on.

London seemed grey and drab after the brilliant tropical colours of the Caribbean, or perhaps it was her own mood which permeated the city streets with dullness. Since the fever had left her she had found herself inhabiting a curious world where nothing seemed to matter; where tiredness surrounded her like a grey pall and where the only emotion she experienced was the sharp pain the merest thought of Zach occasioned.

Her flat was in a small modern block. She had been lucky to get it. Her boss had helped her to obtain the necessary mortgage, and although sometimes meeting the repayments left her shorter of money than she would have wished, she derived considerable satisfaction from knowing that the flat was hers.

The block was surrounded by neatly lawned gardens, randomly landscaped with flowering shrubs and trees; the ancient chestnuts which the builder had had the foresight to leave as a boundary between Tamara's block and that adjacent to it a spectacular backdrop of colour with their new green leaves and deep pink candles.

Gravel crunched under the taxi's wheels as it drew to a halt by the main door. Beneath the block was garaging for residents' cars, although Tamara didn't own one—she could have afforded it, but thought it unnecessary anyway, living as she did in the heart of London.

She paid her fare, surprised when the driver clambered out to carry her cases into the foyer for her.

'You look more like you need a holiday—not as though you've just come back from one,' he told her frankly as she tipped him.

In the lift she glanced in the small mirror. It was true, she did look pale. Her faint tan had faded while she was in hospital and she had also lost weight she could ill afford. Her face had a fragile, vulnerable look about it, her eyes wounded; glazed with a pain they seemed barely able to comprehend.

The eight-hour flight had left her tired and drained, and instead of unpacking she went straight into her bedroom, smoothing clean sheets on the bed she had stripped before going on holiday, then crawling under the duvet where she fell asleep almost the moment her head touched the pillow.

It was dark when she woke up, her mind disorientated, so that it took her several minutes to remember where she was. An oblong of light from the living room bore witness to where she had left a lamp burning and her suitcases lay casually on the floor. She switched on the bedside lamp and glanced at her watch. Three in the morning! Hardly the right time to ring Malcolm and let him know she was back, and she had to go in to the office tomorrow. The authorities on St Stephen's had rung them to explain why her return had been delayed, but still Tamara was not looking forward to the questions she knew her boss would put to her. Even though her body was still tired her mind was too alert for her to be able to go back to sleep. She climbed out of bed and padded around the flat, unpacking her clothes, sorting them into neat piles ready for the washing machine.

People who knew her from the office often expressed surprise when they saw her flat; even Malcolm—not particularly sensitive to his surroundings—had commented rather disapprovingly.

Tamara herself wasn't sure what had prompted her to furnish her small home with soft pastels and natural fabrics—perhaps some dim and distant memory of the happy childhood she had shared with her parents.

Her bedroom was decorated in soft peaches and greens, the wallpaper and fabrics Designers' Guild and horrifically expensive. The small nursing rocking chair had been a junk-shop find which she had stripped and lovingly waxed herself, to match the pine dressing table which had been her first purchase when she bought the flat.

Malcolm's parents' home was furnished with ponderous Victorian antiques, stiff and formal like them, and Tamara had been able to see that when they were married he would expect her to furnish their home in the same style as that favoured by his mother and father.

In the small kitchen Tamara made herself a cup of coffee. The pine units gleamed softly under the pretty lemon-shaded light—the kitchen window overlooked the balcony which ran the length of Tamara's flat with access from the living room, and the windowboxes and plants she had growing there fostered the country atmosphere.

She took her coffee through into the living room—again decorated in her favourite colours, although in here the walls were palest green rather than soft peach; a warm floral fabric in apricots and greens covering the ancient settee Tamara had found on another of her scavenging operations among the local junk-shops.

The stained and polished floor had been her greatest extravagance, brightened up with a rough woven striped rug from Designers' Guild. Tamara loved their fabrics—and their approach, and if other people were amused by the feminine, countrified prettiness of her home she didn't care.

It was her bolthole, her escape from the rest of the world, and she loved it.

In contrast to the femininity of her home the contents of Tamara's wardrobe were bleakly stark; as though all the repression she had learned from her aunt had been swept away in the furnishing of her home, only to reappear when it came to her personal appearance.

For the first time Tamara felt the desire to experiment with more than the basic foundation, eyeshadow and lipstick she kept in her dressing table drawer, and sitting on the tube on her way to work she found herself covertly studying the girls around her, trying to draw comparisons between their appearance and hers. Aunt Lilian had not approved of make-up, 'tarting up your face', she had called it, and while the adult Tamara had acknowledged the narrowness of her aunt's comments, there had still persisted a tiny feeling that make-up should be minimal, utilitarian rather than enhancing, and yet today she found herself wondering if she too could wear that pretty shade of shimmering lilac eyeshadow and that soft pink lipstick.

As she walked down Bond Street her attention strayed to shops in a way it had never done before, especially one displaying an exquisite selection of frivolous underwear. Chain-store undies—and very plain ones at that—had always seemed perfectly adequate to Tamara in the past, and yet now she found herself staring at silk briefs in palest écru, trimmed with satin ribbon. She imagined Zach's fingers on the satin ribbons—on her skin, and then pulled herself up quickly, her face on fire with resentment and embarrassment. What on earth was the matter? She was mooning about like an adolescent or a problem page junkie, imagining that seductive underwear would somehow achieve a miracle and make Zach love her.

'Well, well, you certainly believe in living dangerously!' Tamara knew her boss well enough to respond lightly without committing herself. She had been told by the authorities before she left the island that while her employers had been put in the picture as regards her spider bite nothing had been said about the circumstances in which she had got it except that she had been walking in the rain forest, and Tamara had agreed that that was the way things would stay.

Nigel Soames had been Tamara's boss for three years. They worked well as a team; Tamara cool and controlled, Nigel sometimes erratic but possessed of the verve and flair that made him such an outstanding success in his job, which was the discovery and promotion of new writing talent. The publishers might be an old-established firm, but that did not mean it was old-fashioned; Nigel had had several notable successes in recent years, including an almost but not quite libellous autobiography by a prominent television personality whom Nigel had caught at a vulnerable moment when he had just been refused a plum job and had consequently been in the mood to be far more forthcoming about his colleagues than he might otherwise have been.

Another coup had been a 'faction' novel by a Hong Kong entrepreneur which had reached the best-seller lists in the first few weeks after publication.

Both these and other successes had a habit of draining Nigel of the fierce energy which seemed to burn in him while he was nursing his authors along, and it was Tamara's job to sustain him through the lulls between 'discoveries'.

By the time she had removed her coat she could see that Nigel was on another 'upper'. All the signs were there; the preoccupied, restless manner, the constant pacings of their small office, the incessant coffee drinking and the long abstracted silences, and Tamara blessed Nigel's ability to completely steep himself in whatever he was doing, primarily because it took his attention away from her. Apart from commenting that she didn't look very brown, and calling her 'Miss Muffet', he made very little reference to her absence.

As always when he had a project going, there was no stopping for lunch.

'I think I've hooked him,' he told her enthusiastically, 'and it's going to be a real big one. I can't tell you about it yet.'

Tamara hid a small smile. Nigel had once worked in Fleet Street, and still retained the reporter's instinct for keeping a story to himself until he was ready to commit it to print.

'Would you mind if I rang Malcolm from the office?' Tamara asked him. 'He doesn't know I'm back yet.'

'He doesn't?' He looked at her. 'What's the matter with the man? Why wasn't he waiting at the airport to sweep you off to . . .'

'To his parents' house?' Tamara submitted wryly. 'That isn't Malcolm's style.'

'I know,' Nigel agreed unrepentantly. 'The man's a complete stuffed shirt—a museum specimen. The thing is . . .' he studied Tamara with an abstract gaze, 'this is the first time I've heard you acknowledge as much. Having second thoughts? Holiday romance?'

'Concentrate on your new scoop,' Tamara told him firmly.

'Aha! She doesn't deny it. Now what, I wonder, does that mean?'

'It means,' Tamara told him, refusing to be flustered, 'that like any other woman I like keeping men guessing.'

As Nigel was to tell his wife that evening, it was the first time he could ever remember his cool in-control assistant behaving like a woman. 'She's in love,' he told her, 'you mark my words.'

Pauline Soames, who had met Tamara on several occasions and felt vaguely sorry for her, laughed.

'Of course she is,' she agreed. 'She's engaged, isn't she?'

Tamara knew that Malcolm didn't like her to ring him at his office. Punctilious in such matters, he had once told Tamara that it set a bad example to the rest of the staff, and she, she was appalled to remember, had gravely agreed.

Like a butterfly emerging from a chrysalis she could hardly reconcile the repressed, unresponsive creature she had been with the woman Zach had brought to life.

Malcolm's secretary, the daughter of friends of his parents, with an almost painfully upper-class voice, informed her that Malcolm was still in New York.

'He'll be ringing me this afternoon,' she added. 'Can I give him a message?'

Having asked her to ask Malcolm to call her as soon as he could Tamara went back to work. At four o'clock Nigel announced that he had had enough. Since he had spent the last thirty-five minutes doodling on his blotter and staring at the phone with a concentration that could have fractured steel, Tamara could only conclude that matters were not going according to plan.

'Shall I hang on, just in case?' she offered, glancing at the phone. 'If you're expecting a call.'

'I was, but something tells me it won't be coming through—not today anyway. No, you go home, Tamara. You look all in,' he told her untactfully. 'Completely washed out.'

She did, Tamara acknowledged ruefully ten minutes later, as she examined her reflection in the cloakroom mirror.

It was that time of the day when most of the afternoon shoppers were on their way home and the commuters had yet to leave their offices, and so Bond Street was relatively empty as she walked down it heading for her Tube station.

Today, for some reason, the Elizabeth Arden salon which she had passed almost every day for the last few years without sparing a second glance seemed to draw her attention as she remembered the faces of the attractively made up girls she had seen that morning and compared them with hers.

Without being aware of moving she had stepped inside. Had the girl behind the reception desk been more intimidating and less attractive she would probably have fled, but to her astonishment she found her tentative enquiries answered with a reassuring smile and the information that she was lucky—they had a cancellation and one of their make-up experts could give her a lesson right away.

Something she had not expected was that the 'expert' would be male; and an extremely attractive male at that.

When she had accepted his invitation to sit down he studied Tamara's face in absolute silence for several minutes before pronouncing,

'Your bone structure is excellent and like many Englishwomen you have a good skin, but you've neglected it. This blue eyeshadow is far too hard for you.'

With deft movements he removed the make-up Tamara had applied, leaving her skin soft and supple, turning to a vast array of cosmetics concealed in the clinically clean units lining the small make-up room.

'First we use foundation—not the sort you were using. It's too thick—too heavy. Your skin must breathe, that way its true beauty will show through.'

He applied the make-up with a damp sponge, so thinly that Tamara was astonished to see how the liquid transformed her skin, giving it a soft pearly sheen.

The hour that followed was a revelation. She could hardly believe that the infinitesimal amount of soft lilac eyeshadow Pierre used had been all it took to make her eyes seem so large and almost amethyst in colour.

'Subtlety is the key,' Pierre advised her warningly. 'Your eyes are magnificent—like the eyes of a startled fawn. Before you leave I will de your lashes for you; they're dark already, but darkening them a shade further will help to dramatise their size.'

Blusher gleamed softly along cheekbones suddenly far more prominent than Tamara remembered, a soft slick of lipstick as pretty as any worn by the girls she had seen that morning completing the effect.

With the help of the chart Pierre had done for her, she was able to purchase new make-up in the boutique, and Pierre's final words rang in her ears as she hurried out into the now busy streets.

'Wear your hair down,' he had instructed her. 'It's far too beautiful to be scraped back into that ugly knot. If you must wear it up choose a softer style.'

She would experiment with it tonight, she promised herself, hoping it would not be an impossible task for her to master the techniques Pierre had shown her.

Further down Bond Street she lingered by the lingerie shop she had seen that morning, one half of her warning her scornfully that nothing she could do would bring Zach back, while the other—the new feminine half—yearned for the soft sensuality of silk and satin against the skin that could still remember every feverish second when the male warmth of Zach's body had been its only covering.

In the end she went in rather hesitantly. The boutique was empty of other customers and a pleasant girl came forward to ask if she needed any help.

'The bra and briefs in the window,' Tamara began nervously, 'I . . .'

'They're gorgeous, aren't they?' the girl enthused, smiling. 'I've been drooling over them myself. They're new stock.' She glanced at Tamara's hand. 'Perfect for a honeymoon. There's a nightdress and matching negligee. Let me show them to you.'

The gossamer-fine silk rippled over the counter, the delicate insets of lace adding to the cobwebby effect.

'Try them on,' the girl urged.

Telling herself that she was being an absolute fool, Tamara stepped into the small cubicle. The nightdress, so demure off, had a surprising sensuality on, and not merely in the silky brush of the fabric against her skin. The lace insets revealed a considerable amount of pearly flesh; the shoestring straps which tied in tiny bows were deliberately provocative.

When she left the shop half an hour later Tamara could still not believe that she had parted with such an exorbitant sum of money in such a lost cause. Her face flamed with the knowledge of her deceit. The girl had thought she was buying the clothes for the delectation of her 'fiancé', but Tamara knew that there was only one man she wanted to see her in that drift of silk and lace; only one man's hands she desired to unfasten those satin bows and press seductive kisses in their place, and it certainly wasn't Malcolm.

That was when she knew beyond any shadow of a doubt that she would have to terminate her engagement. In the rain forest she had used it as a means of self-defence to prevent Zach from thinking that she was trying to trap him into a more permanent relationship than he wanted, but she was not in the rain forest now, and Malcolm would have to be told the truth—or at least enough of the truth to convince him that their engagement was over.

She had just gone to bed when her telephone started to ring, her first illogical thought that it might be Zach quenched when she realised that even if he wanted to get in touch with her he didn't know where she lived.

When she picked up the receiver the voice she heard was Dot's, ringing to check up that she was all right.

'I'm fine,' Tamara told her lightly, 'so fine in fact that I've just spent a fortune on new make-up and clothes.'

'Good for you!'

Dot sounded genuinely approving. They chatted for a few minutes and then she hung up, having reminded Tamara that she was more than welcome to pay them a visit.

It was a novel experience for Tamara to have someone so concerned about her. She had always maintained a slight distance with people, never allowing them to come too close—until now, and she had let Zach come dangerously close and like a moth she was destined to be irreparably hurt by the thing that attracted her the most.

She had barely replaced the receiver when the telephone rang again. This time it was Malcolm.

'Who was that on the phone when I rang five minutes ago?' he asked her crossly, not at all mollified when she explained.

'Karen tells me you want to speak to me?'

Not a word of concern for her, Tamara noticed critically, quelling the thought as disloyal. She had never found fault with Malcolm in the past and he was hardly to blame for exhibiting the very characteristics which had drawn her to him in the first place. Had she questioned him about it she had no doubt that he would have replied huffily that if she had not been fully recovered he would not have expected her to return home in the first place.

'Yes, I did,' she agreed. 'When do you hope to come home?'

'By the weekend. I've arranged for us to go and stay with the parents. You'll be able to tell them all about your holiday. Not that they approve,' he warned her. 'Mother doesn't think it's a good idea for people to holiday separately.'

'Malcolm, must we?' she began desperately. 'There's something I want to discuss with you . . .'

'Well, we can discuss it at the weekend. The parents always give us plenty of time together.'

Deliberately contrived half-hours last thing at night which left Tamara feeling acutely selfconscious and stiffly unresponsive when Malcolm did take advantage of his parents' 'tactful' disappearance to kiss her.

'Malcolm, this isn't something I . . .'

'Look, Tam,' he broke in, using the diminutive which she hated, 'I can't talk now. I'll pick you up at the usual time on Friday. We'll have plenty of time to discuss whatever it is. I must go.'

Why had she never realised before how stuffy and pompous he was? Tamara asked herself.

Knowing Malcolm's fetish for punctuality she was ready well in advance of eight-thirty. She had packed enough clothes to take her through the weekend—a silk jersey dress for dinner on Saturday—the Mellors always dressed for dinner. The dress was a new one; a silver lilac shade which did things she had never dreamed possible for her eyes and figure.

Taking Pierre's advice, she had started to wear her hair loose and had even paid a visit to the hairdressing salon favoured by some of the other girls at work where the ends had been trimmed and some of the excess weight removed, leaving her hair to curl softly in a gently shaped bell. She was even beginning to master the intricacies of her new make-up, and felt justifiably proud of herself as she caught sight of her reflection in the mirror.

The Caribbean sun had bleached her hair slightly; her new misty mauve eyeshadow added haunting depths to her eyes, the soft iced raspberry lipstick outlined the warm curves of her mouth.

To travel in she was wearing something completely different for her, a pair of casual cotton trousers cut in the latest style—a pretty shade of lilac with a toning striped blouson and a matching reefer jacket.

Malcolm arrived sharp on the dot of eight-thirty, the expression of disapproval in his eyes as he looked at Tamara almost ludicrous.

'You can't mean to travel dressed like that?' he complained.

'Why not?' Tamara retorted coolly. 'It's comfortable and I like it.'

'You look like a teenager,' Malcolm accused, but she refused to be swayed. Women far older than her dressed equally casually, and after all, didn't she have the right to rescue what she could from those flat sterile years when living with Aunt Lilian had stolen from her the natural spontaneity of youth?

In a disapproving silence Malcolm carried her case down to his BMW. Tamara knew that he hated her to talk while he was driving, and as the powerful car ate up the miles she found her tension steadily increasing. If only she had been able to tell him in London that she wanted to end their engagement! If only she wasn't going to be forced to tell him while they were at his parents'. She had toyed with the idea of waiting until they returned, but her innate sense of honesty compelled her to tell him as soon as she could; she could not stay under his parents' roof under false pretences, and besides, now that she had made up her mind she longed for the whole thing to be over and done with.

The Mellors' house was set in the Cotswolds, 'Young Royals Country', as Mrs Mellors was snobbishly fond of describing it.

Malcolm's parents were waiting to greet them when they arrived. There was the normal ritual of sherry in the drawing room. Tamara had not missed the way Malcolm's mother had examined her reflection and it gave her an impish sense of amusement to guess that she was thinking how unsuitable Tamara was as a wife for her son. No doubt she would prefer the elegant Karen who came from the 'right' background.

'Well, we'll leave you young things together,' the Colonel said with a heavy gallantry that grated on Tamara's nerves. Of the two she preferred Malcolm's father, but it was a daunting thought to realise that in thirty years' time Malcolm would be almost an exact replica of him. 'No doubt you'll want to tell Malcolm all about your holiday, Tamara.'

'Such a dreadful experience for you!' Mrs Mellors exclaimed. 'I remember when Humphrey was stationed in Ceylon one had to be so careful. Personally I've never cared for hot climates—so unhealthy and unhygienic. I never thought it was wise your going off on your own like that. And walking in that rain forest . . .'

'Come along, my dear,' the Colonel interrupted hastily. 'We'll see you both in the morning.'

The drawing-room felt stuffy and oppressive. Tamara could smell the lily of the valley scent Malcolm's mother used and she longed to suggest that they walk in the garden. Perhaps there she would find it easier to say what had to be said.

'I think Mother is quite right, you know,' Malcolm began in aggrieved tones, as he poured himself another glass of sherry. 'I never cared for the idea of you going off like that, but you would insist.'

'In other words, being bitten by a spider served me right, is that it?' Tamara asked him dryly. Why had she never realised before how spoiled and at times downright childish he was?

'Well, you must admit it wouldn't have happened if you'd stayed at home.'

'Like a dutiful fiancée?' Suddenly the task ahead of her didn't seem anywhere near as daunting as it had, and she mentally thanked Malcolm for unwittingly making it easier for her.

'Malcolm, there's something I have to tell you.' She slid the solitaire off her finger, noticing that it had become quite loose—a result of her illness, no doubt. 'I think we should break off our engagement. I don't think it's the right step for either of us. You need a wife who will be a social asset—someone like Karen. I don't really fit in.'

'Perhaps not, but you could learn,' Malcolm told her with a tactlessness that astounded her. 'Mother will be able to give you some good pointers.'

'Malcolm, I don't think you understand,' she told him with weary patience. 'It isn't a question of whether I could "learn" to be the sort of wife you want, it's simply that I no longer want to be that sort of person.'

He had started to go a dull red.

'You mean you've met someone else—indulged in some cheap shoddy affair while you were away, is that it?'

He was close enough to the truth for it to be painful, although Tamara managed to say valiantly, 'It was neither cheap nor shoddy on my part, but yes, if you want to put it that way.'

'You'll regret it. We could have had a good life together,' he told her, but Tamara noticed that he no longer attempted to dissuade her.

'There's just one thing,' he added.

Tamara waited.

'Can we leave things as they stand at the moment? The parents have invited a neighbour over for dinner tomorrow. He's something of a big noise locally, and it would upset them . . .'

'And your mother's table arrangements?' Tamara suggested wryly.

'You owe me that at least,' Malcolm pressed on doggedly. 'My parents are bound to know that it's you who broke off our engagement if I tell them this weekend—I'd hardly bring you down here if it was a mutual arrangement—so I'd prefer to wait to announce the news to them until after we get back to London.'

In the circumstances Tamara could hardly refuse. With great reluctance and even greater distaste she slid the solitaire back on her finger.

At least Malcolm had accepted her decision without argument—had perhaps been secretly relieved by it.

'So that's settled, then,' Malcolm exclaimed in evident relief. 'Good—I don't want Zachary Fletcher laughing at me behind my back. I had enough of that when we were at school.'

Tamara felt as though all the breath had been dragged out of her lungs. It was fortunate that Malcolm wasn't looking at her at that moment, because had he been, he must surely have realised the truth.

'Zachary Fletcher?' Did her voice actually tremble as much as it seemed to do to her?

'Yes. He lives several miles away—he inherited a great barn of a place from his uncle. He was in the Army for a while, I don't know what he's doing with himself at the moment. The only reason the

parents have invited him over is because they hope
to persuade him to allow the hunt over his land.'
He glanced at his watch. 'I'm going up to bed.
Remember, Tamara, as far as everyone else is concerned we're still engaged—at least until this weekend is over.'

. Alone in the drawing room, Tamara suppressed
the waves of hysterical laughter bubbling up inside
her.

Of all the cruel ironies of fate! Zachary Fletcher
a close neighbour of Malcolm's parents. She and
Zachary Fletcher facing one another across Mrs
Mellors heavy Victorian dining table making
polite conversation; Zachary Fletcher, who had
promised he would never tell her fiancé what had
happened. Zachary Fletcher, who must *not* discover that she had broken her engagement in case
he thought it was because she expected something
from him!

CHAPTER SEVEN

ZACHARY here! Even now Tamara could hardly believe it. She knew he had arrived, because she had heard the purr of a car across the gravel outside and then the ring of the front doorbell.

She had spent the day in a constant state of tension; it was just as well that neither of Malcolm's parents were in the least perceptive, otherwise they must have surely realised that something was wrong.

She and Malcolm had gone for a walk after lunch—the Mellors were firm believers in the beneficial effect of fresh air and Tamara had been urged outside to 'get some colour back into her face,' as Malcolm's mother put it, adding rather maliciously that perhaps it was the new make-up Tamara was affecting that had had such a disastrous result on her complexion.

Tamara had bitten hard on her tongue and told herself that this was the last weekend she would have to spend with Malcolm's parents and surely she could endure it without quarrelling with them. A walk had been the last thing she had felt like after lunch—in point of fact she had felt decidedly queasy. The Mellors were fond of rich food and Tamara had noticed a tendency to nausea since her return from the Caribbean and put it down to the after-effects of her illness. The island doctor had explained to her that the poison injected by the spider had very similar properties to modern paralysing drugs, combined with a powerful numbing effect similar to a tranquilliser. He had also made it frighteningly clear to her just how close she had come to losing her life; telling her that if it hadn't been for Zachary's prompt action she would have died.

And now, having told herself that it was over and that he was gone from her life, she was to see him again. The very thought was enough to make her fingers tremble violently as she tried to apply her make-up.

Oh God, she thought wearily, she could not go down there and face him. She couldn't! But she had to. If she disappeared now and by some mischance Zach mentioned that he too had been on St Stephen's at the same time as she had been there, Malcolm was bound to put two and two together and come to the conclusion that her departure—and possibly the termination of their engagement—had something to do with Zach, and Tamara could not bear that to happen. If was bad enough having to cope with the anguish of knowing that Zach despised her, without having him realise that she had fallen in love with him.

And so, she forced herself to concentrate on the task of applying her make-up as Pierre had so painstakingly taught her—not make-up but warpaint, she thought half hysterically. Warpaint to make her look braver than she was.

The Mellors were sticklers for punctuality and knowing this Tamara was ready on the dot of eight, wearing her new silver-lavender dress, her face carefully made up and her nails frosted a soft rose, her hair cascading to her shoulders in a sleek bell.

In the doorway she paused and then re-traced her steps, with a final flourish of bravado spraying the outrageously expensive perfume she had bought for herself on the pulse points at her wrists, throat and the backs of her knees, and then as a last thought picked up a silver mesh shawl to drape round her shoulders, as she knew from chilly experience that the Mellors were careful of their heating bills and often the large drawing room could be almost cold, especially when one was sitting down.

The others were already in the drawing room. Tina, the girl from the village who came up to help Mrs Briggs with the cooking and serve the meals when the Mellors entertained, was proffering a glass of sherry to Zach, her expression almost fatuously bemused.

No one had seen Tamara yet and she had a cowardly impulse to leave now and damn the consequences, and then Malcolm looked up and came towards her. Formal clothes became his rather too solid frame, his fair hair gleaming under the lights.

'Ah, there you are, darling!' he exclaimed, curving her towards him with an unexpectedly proprietorial air. 'Umm, you smell nice, what is it?'

'L'Heure Bleue,' Tamara replied automatically, her eyes leaping the chasm that lay beyond herself and Zach, her feelings clearly betrayed in them for a brief second before she caught herself up and turned away to accept a glass of dry sherry from Tina, with a composure that half of her unwillingly admired while the other half stood aside and mocked that it could not possibly last.

'What a pretty frock, my dear,' Malcolm's mother exclaimed, 'and such an unusual colour. I don't believe I've seen you wearing it before. In my day engaged girls didn't work as they do nowadays, of course, but I can still remember saving my pin money to buy things for my bottom drawer. Of course, things are very different now . . .'

How would she have felt if she genuinely loved Malcolm? Tamara wondered wryly. As mothers-in-law went, hers would certainly have been a formidable adversary.

'Zachary,' Colonel Mellors interrupted, 'let me introduce you to our daughter-in-law to be. Tamara my dear, meet Zachary Fletcher, one of our closest neighbours.'

'Mr Fletcher.'

Again she marvelled at the even tone of her voice; at the cool steadiness of her fingers as they barely touched Zach's, her eyes sliding warily away.

'Tamara—I'm afraid I shall have to call you that as Colonel Mellors hasn't told me your surname.'

There was mockery and something else—less kind—a kind of hard inflexibility underlining the words, but no one else seemed to be aware of the suddenly charged atmosphere which was to colour the entire evening like a tautly drawn glittering thread in a skein of dull grey wool.

Merely his presence was like an electric charge, Tamara admitted when they went into the dining room.

Malcolm's parents were talking about the iniquities of income tax, and the problems of leaving one's possessions to one's families.

'Of course, Malcolm will take over from us here one day. Mellors have owned this land since the time of Queen Victoria.'

'And how does Tamara feel about living in the country?' Zach asked carelessly, his question voiced to the Colonel, but his eyes on Tamara herself.

'Oh, she knows that Malcolm would simply not countenance living anywhere else,' Mrs Mellors cut in before anyone else could speak. 'And of course it is still a woman's duty to live her husband's life rather than vice versa.'

'Whither thou goest?' Zach quoted, his eyes still on Tamara's faintly flushed face. 'An ideological and often impossible belief. You have no career, then, Tamara? No ambitions of your own?'

He was deliberately trying to goad her, Tamara realised with a sudden shock of pain that even now after all that had happened he was still trying to hurt her.

'There's no need for Tamara to have ambitions,' Malcolm's mother told Zach firmly. 'Of course it's a pity that she refuses to hunt.' Having turned the conversation on to the topic which was the purpose of the meal, all three Mellors now discussed the merits of hunting enthusiastically, breaking off now and again to ask Zach's opinion, which was always given in a pleasant but carefully noncommittal tone, which told them nothing, either of his personal views or his intentions with regard to the hunt's access over his land.

'Well, I suggest that we males retire to my study with the port,' the Colonel declared genially when the meal drew to a close. 'It will give the girls a chance to make wedding plans, eh, Tamara?'

Needless to say they did nothing of the kind, in fact Mrs Mellors sedulously avoided the subject, and it gave Tamara a certain amount of grim satisfaction to know that little though she realised it, Mrs Mellors was about to be granted her greatest wish.

Pleading a headache, Tamara excused herself when the men finally joined them. She suspected from the Colonel's darkly crimson expression that all had not gone as well as he had anticipated, and this was borne out when Tamara heard Zachary saying coolly,

'Yes, I'm sure you're right, Colonel, and far be it from me to spoil any man's sport, but I have plans for my land which do not include the hunting of foxes all over it.'

Upstairs in her room Tamara started to prepare for bed, running her bath while she started to undress. The silk jersey dress fell to the floor, where she let it lie unregarded. Coming into the room afresh, she had caught the elusive echo of her own fragrance, and was startled by its alien sophistication and the image it projected; the image which was now hers.

It there was one thing and one thing alone she had gained from knowing Zach, it was the sheer pleasure of sensuality. Her silk camiknickers had been another frivolous present to herself. She had read that they were all the rage in America, where for some reason they referred to them as 'teddies.' These were silver grey to match the sheer silk stockings she had bought to wear with her new dress. She was just starting to clean off her make-up when she heard the tap of her door, and picking up her robe from the bed, she went to open it. The last thing she wanted now was an argument with Malcolm. The headache which had originally been fiction was fast becoming fact.

As she opened the door she said wearily, 'Oh, Malcolm, please—not tonight . . .'

'My, my, things have changed since St Stephen's!' came the drawling taunt from the doorway, as Zachary Fletcher stepped across it.

If an evening suit became Malcolm, it turned

Zach into a virile demigod. Tamara stepped back instinctively, panic fluttering in the pit of her stomach as she acknowledged the danger he represented to her fragile defences.

'You're certainly a creature of surprises,' Zach continued, stepping past her into the room and turning to close the door, which he then proceeded to lean against, effectively blocking her exit, arms folded across his chest. 'What happened? Or can I guess? Having lost your virginity to me, you had to discover some other means of keeping Malcolm interested, so you swopped from innocence to world-weary experience, and he, poor fool, couldn't tell that your newly found "experience" was gained in the arms of another man. Clever, aren't you, but a word of warning. Your estimable mama-in-law to be isn't fooled, and she doesn't want to see you married to her one and only.'

'It's what Malcolm and I want that matters,' Tamara flung at him tightly, anger superseding the shock his words had originally caused her.

'And Malcolm wants you? No wonder!' Zach drawled insultingly. 'Dressed like that you're every adolescent's dream of a centre-fold come to life.'

The sound of her palm across his jaw filled the room, leaving Tamara white and sick, hating herself for the violence he had forced her into.

'Oh, come on,' Zach mocked, ignoring the red flush marking the brown skin. 'What did you have in mind? A little visual titillation to follow up that bored, "Not tonight?" I'll just bet the poor so-and-so doesn't even know what's hit him. He's the type that thinks women come in two varieties—the ones you marry and the ones you go to bed with. No doubt he thinks he's got the bargain of the decade in you—both in one sweet-smelling, tantalisingly wrapped package. So tantalising in fact that I'm tempted to unwrap a little of it myself.'

'Get out!' Tamara snapped at him through gritted teeth. 'Just get out of here!'

This was a thousand times worse than anything she had visualised even in her worst moments; despite the smiling lips the jade eyes were as cold and empty as glass. Tamara could sense within him an unrelenting anger, and it was that that made her retreat, trying not to betray the effect he had upon her.

'When I'm ready,' he told her softly, adding almost conversationally, 'Do you know that since I made love to you there hasn't been a day when I haven't regretted robbing your husband-to-be of the privilege of being the "first." I even wondered if what had happened between us might somehow make you feel guilty enough to break off your engagement—it isn't unknown. But I needn't have worried, need I, Tamara? A scheming little bitch like you soon found a way to turn circumstances to her own advantage.'

'Scheming? I prefer to think of myself as resourceful,' Tamara lied tightly. 'Why did you come up here? So that you could self-righteously denounce me to Malcolm?'

'What's the matter? Frightened he might break the engagement if I do?' Zach sneered.

His contempt seemed to unleash a reckless torrent of rage inside Tamara, so strong that she no longer cared what she risked; what she did.

'What makes you think Malcolm would want to break it?' she threw at him tauntingly. 'Perhaps he prefers me more with the experience than he did without it!'

The whole of Zach's body seemed to stiffen and

harden, and through her elation at having at last got through to him Tamara felt the first beginnings of prickling fear.

'Well, in that case,' he murmured smoothly, 'perhaps I ought to give you some more.'

He moved so quickly that she hadn't a chance of escape. Her robe was thrust ruthlessly aside, his fingers biting into her shoulders as his mouth came down on hers in a savagely brutal kiss, the touch of his hands on her body, drawing whimpers of pain into a throat raw with tears, her mind reeling from the knowledge that this was the reverse coin of the passion they had shared before; this was passion with a sadistic face, and yet mindlessly her body still responded to its primitive call, her hands locking behind Zachary's neck, her slim form pressing pleadingly against the hard muscles of his.

When he wrenched his mouth away they were both trembling; Zach with anger, and Tamara with desire.

'You little bitch,' he said thickly. 'You enjoyed that, didn't you?'

Sickly Tamara stared at him, knowing that even if she wanted to she could never make him understand. Her mind knew that he had deliberately insulted and degraded her, but her body knew only that his was the touch it craved and could make no distinction between punishment and pleasure.

'Tamara, can I come in?'

She froze as she heard Malcolm's voice, and reached unsteadily for her robe, avoiding the curling mouth and hard eyes of the man watching her, suddenly remembering that she had left the bath water running.

'Just a moment,' she called back, hurrying into the bathroom to turn off the tap, before going to open her bedroom door. Let Zach make whatever excuses he wanted for being in her room; she no longer cared; no doubt he thought to humiliate her and hurt her as well, but the only person he would hurt was Malcolm, and little though she wanted that to happen she knew enough about her ex-fiancé to know that the blow would be to his pride rather than his emotions.

'I wanted to talk to you about last night,' Malcolm began as he walked in, then the sudden shock of discovering Zachary leaning against the wall was enough to produce a silence and then a heavy frown as he looked first at Zach and then at Tamara herself.

'What . . .'

'I asked your mother which was Tamara's room,' Zach explained smoothly. 'She left this downstairs.' Miraculously he produced the gauzy scarf which Tamara had indeed left downstairs, 'and I was just returning it to her.'

'I can't think why Mother didn't simply say she would return the scarf to you,' Malcolm complained when they were alone. 'Odd sort of chap, don't you think? Now, Tam, about last night,' he began again when Tamara made no response.

'There's nothing to say,' she told him firmly. 'Our engagement is off, Malcolm, and if you're honest with yourself, you'll admit that it's best that way.'

She compounded the unpleasantness of the weekend by over-sleeping on Sunday morning, and so missing church. Malcolm's mother made her disapproval plain when they returned, adding that once Malcolm and Tamara came to live in the Cotswolds, it would be Tamara's duty to set the villagers an example by going to church. All in all

Tamara was not sorry to return to the solitude of her own flat.

She had given Malcolm his ring back in the car. He made no suggestion that they should meet again or that Tamara should reconsider, and she guessed that he would soon find solace elsewhere—possibly with the far more suitable Karen.

The main topic of the return journey to London had, to Tamara's dismay, been Zach.

Malcolm appeared to have taken a violent dislike to him, for some reason that Tamara could not fathom. From Malcolm she learned that Zach had recently inherited his uncle's estate and the large house that went with it.

'He just isn't our sort,' Malcolm complained. 'His mother was on the stage.'—Malcolm made it sound an unpardonable lapse of taste. 'And the last thing we heard about him was that he was in the Army.'

'Well, surely your father approved of that,' Tamara interposed.

'I suppose he would have done if he'd made anything of it, but he got chucked out, and ever since then he's been bumming around.'

Tamara wondered what Malcolm would say if she told him that far from 'bumming around' as Malcolm so contemptuously accused, Zach had been with the S.A.S., but wisely she refrained from doing so.

On the Monday morning when she got up for work, a wave of giddiness almost made her lose her balance, and the thought of food of any kind was totally nauseating.

Tamara blamed it on the tension of the weekend, and the heavy food she had eaten.

Nigel remarked that she looked too pale for someone who had been away on holiday and told her that she ought to get her doctor to check her over.

'Better be on the safe side,' he told her firmly. 'You never know with these tropical fevers . . .'

'Thanks—I was bitten by a spider, remember,' she told him, 'not stricken with Lassa fever!'

Nigel grinned. He was wearing his 'I'm into something big' again face, and walked out of the office whistling off-key, a sure sign that things were beginning to jell. It was Tamara's conviction that Nigel enjoyed the hunt for a new talent more than the surefire success books that resulted from it.

Although she had scoffed at his advice, when a week went by and she was feeling no better, she decided that it might be as well to have a check up. She belonged to a large group practice, and the busy doctor who saw her was brusque and to the point.

'There's nothing wrong with you,' he told her dryly, having examined her thoroughly and asked a good many questions, 'unless you count pregnancy as an illness. I'll have to test to make sure, but I'm ninety per cent certain you're in the early stages of pregnancy. If you are and you want a termination . . .'

'No!'

The word was out without her having to think about it, and for the first time she received a faintly approving smile.

'Come back in a fortnight's time and we'll talk again. The results of the test will be through in about a week. Ring my receptionist to check, and if, as I suspect, you are pregnant she'll start making arrangements for ante-natal care, relaxation classes, all that sort of thing.'

Tamara left the surgery in a daze. Pregnant! She could barely take it in. The signs had been there, but she naïvely had not perceived them; it had simply not occurred to her that as a result of Zach's lovemaking she might conceive his child. Zach's child! She came to an abrupt halt, torn between wildly fluctuating joy and pain—joy because she would bear the child of the man she loved, and pain because he would never know of its existence.

It was only later that the agonising started; did she have the right to bring up her child alone, depriving it of the love it could receive from two parents were it adopted; did she have the right to have the baby at all?

'Everything okay?' Nigel asked her, coming into her office as she was removing her coat, and frowning slightly when he saw her dazed expression.

'Tamara?'

'I'm pregnant,' she told him baldly.

'Pregnant?' He did an obvious double-take and stared. 'Hell! I suppose that means you'll be bringing the date of the wedding forward, and I'll lose you right in the middle of the biggest thing that's ever happened to this firm!'

Tamara tried not to laugh. He was the supreme egotist.

'There won't be any wedding,' she told him quietly, holding out her left hand. 'Look, no ring.'

'But after this!' Nigel expostulated. 'Hell, even a prune like Malcolm couldn't leave you high and dry with his child!'

'Wrong and wrong again.' It was amazing how cheerful she managed to sound. 'One, the baby isn't Malcolm's, and two, I was the one to break the engagement—before I knew about the baby.

Not that knowing would have altered my decision. If I couldn't marry Malcolm because I didn't love him I certainly couldn't marry him to give a name to someone else's child.'

'I see.' For once all Nigel's attention was focused on her. He perched on the end of her desk, toying with a pencil. 'Umm, I'd noticed a certain . . . blossoming of late, a certain honing of features which had always been there, but neglected so to speak. So. Well, are you planning to marry the man who's the father of your child?'

Tamara shook her head.

'It was a very brief encounter,' she said lightly. 'I loved him; he desired me. The fact that I'm pregnant is not his concern. What I would like to know is, will you keep me on?'

It cost a lot to speak so matter-of-factly, but it had to be done.

'I don't see why not, but it won't be easy for you,' Nigel warned her, 'especially not once the baby has been born. I know enough about you, Tamara, to know that you're not the sort of woman who'll want to let anyone else bring up her child, but still at least you've got your own home, and I suppose we could come to some flexible arrangement over hours; perhaps you could even work at home part of the time . . .'

Tamara had to turn away to hide the quick rush of grateful tears. She had still not really taken in the fact that she was pregnant; it had all happened too quickly.

'This man,' Nigel was saying, 'you met him in the Caribbean, I take it. You say you love him—are you sure it's not just infatuation? Malcolm might not be the most exciting man on earth, but . . .'

Tamara shook her head decisively.

'No. To both questions.'

'Mm—well, I know when I've met a lady who knows her own mind. Which reminds me—talking of people who know their own minds, I've managed to fix up an interview for my next project. It's definitely going to be a biggie, Tamara. We're driving down to see him next Friday. Lunch at his stately pile,' he grinned, enjoying her expression. 'You're about to meet a philanthropist. He wants to turn his home into a rehabilitation centre for disturbed children, and the book is going to help finance it.'

'What's the book going to be about?' Tamara asked him.

'Faction—but this time it's all about power games. He's a very shrewd operator, knowledgeable in his field too, but he's determined not to sell himself cheap.'

'He sounds formidable,' Tamara said lightly. 'Will you want me to make notes or will you use the recorder?'

'We might as well be prepared for both. From the outline he's sent me I don't think there'll be too much to discuss. He read English Literature at Cambridge and he certainly seems to know how to put his point across.'

The rest of the day passed in a blur of telephone calls, checking on the progress of a jacket cover for a children's book they had in hand, and soothing the affronted feelings of a writer who had been trying to speak to Nigel for a week without success, and it wasn't until she was back in her own flat that Tamara could give her mind over to the reality of her pregnancy. She touched her stomach—still flat, showing no sign of the life growing inside her.

Zach's child. Illogically, she wanted a son. But she must not smother the child, whatever sex it was, she warned herself. She must remember always that it would probably inherit some of Zach's fierce independence—an independence it would surely need. But one-parent families were no longer remarkable.

It never even occurred to her to try to get in touch with Zach. If he knew about the baby it would only be an embarrassment to him. He would probably advise her to obtain an abortion; he might even drawl in that same hatefully mocking voice he had used the last time she had seen him that the paternity was in doubt and that the baby might possibly be Malcolm's.

No, it was far better that he didn't know.

The flat had a second small bedroom which she used as a storeroom-cum-study; she could use it for the baby. It was a pity there was no proper garden, but there was a park within walking distance, and perhaps later she could buy a small house . . . For the first time since she had returned from the Caribbean she felt that she had some purpose in life; something to live for instead of merely existing. Zach could never be hers, but his child . . .

She was smiling when she went to bed, but while she slept tears slid down her cheeks. Having Zach's baby was a bitter-sweet pleasure, knowing that his father would never be there to see him growing up.

CHAPTER EIGHT

A WEEK later Nigel announced that the following day, which was a Friday, they were going to visit their new author.

'Not that he's committed himself to us yet,' Nigel admitted, 'but I'm hoping to get something concrete out of him this afternoon, so smile your sweetest at him.'

Tamara merely smiled. She knew when she was being teased, and yet she could not help feeling a tiny glow of pride early the next morning when Nigel came to pick her up at her flat, his eyes widening as she came towards him.

She had dressed carefully for their visit. When Aunt Lilian had died she had left Tamara her house and the money which had come to her on Tamara's parents' death and which she had carefully put aside for her great-niece, and although previously Tamara had not given much thought to the matter she was grateful now to have the quite substantial sum behind her. The only money she had spent since her aunt's death had been on buying the flat, but since her return from holiday, in the brief weeks before discovering her pregnancy she had surprised herself by almost completely renovating her wardrobe. Today's outfit was one of the results, and it was the first time it had been warm enough to wear the petrol blue suit with its contrasting white blouse.

The clothes were from a range of separates

Tamara had discovered in a small boutique, and the skirt had caught her eye immediately. Basically quite plain, it had been made attractively eyecatching by the addition of self-coloured embroidery just below the neat wasitline, and an insert of tiny fan pleats in the front seam. The blouse was decorated with appliquéd satin flowers on the shoulders and yoke, and Tamara knew that the outfit was both demure and feminine.

'Very nice,' Nigel approved. 'And I like your hair too. It looks much better down. Makes you look more approachable somehow.'

'Not too approachable, I hope,' Tamara retaliated teasingly.

By rights she ought to have been feeling terrible. Here she was expecting a child and unmarried—Aunt Lilian would have been disgusted and horrified, but all Tamara could feel was intense joy. It was as though knowing she was carrying Zach's child helped to ease the aching pain of his absence. She wasn't looking through rose-coloured glasses, though. She knew there would be hard times ahead, times when she regretted intensely committing herself to single parenthood, but there would also be great joy, a new dimension to life.

'Wake up, dreamer!' Nigel chided her, opening his car door.

Tamara settled herself composedly. It was by no means unusual for her to visit authors with Nigel. Their firm believed in pampering its authors and frequently, rather than subject them to the harrowing journey to London, they visited them in their own homes. Normally Tamara remained very much in the background, notebook on hand, listening carefully for anything that Nigel might forget.

They took the M4 towards Bristol. The motorway was relatively quiet, 'Too early for weekend escapers,' Nigel told her. Outside the car windows the countryside basked in a rare day of June sunshine. Tiny white clouds scudded storybook fashion across a sky the shade of blue which is only found in England, and Tamara leaned back in her seat and enjoyed the intense sensation of wellbeing she was experiencing.

At Bristol they turned on to the M5 to head north, the Bristol Channel to their left and the beginnings of hills to their right.

Gloucester was their first town, and as they travelled down one particularly wide and gracious street Tamara was reminded that it had once been a famous spa to rival Bath and Tunbridge Wells, and her mind mentally populated the curving terrace of Regency houses with dandies tooling dangerously fast carriages, and demure damsels in floating muslin dresses and huge poke bonnets.

The Cotswolds were familiar to her from her visits to see Malcolm's parents, but she never tired of the enchantment of rounding a corner and coming upon a tiny village, or of the green and gold patchwork of fields.

'Not far now,' Nigel told her, mistaking her sigh of pleasure for one of tiredness. 'We're looking for a village with the improbable name of Wharton-under-the-Hill. There should be a signpost on your left any moment now.'

They came to it several seconds later, taking a meandering B-road along leafy lanes, heavy with cow-parsley and ragged Robin. Wild roses were blooming in the hedgerows and Tamara wound down her window to breathe in the sweet summer air. Despite Malcolm's mother's oft-voiced beliefs

to the contrary, Tamara did like the country, and
at this particular moment could think of nothing
more delightful than settling down in one of the
tiny huddle of cottages which comprised the village
of Wharton. The 'under-the-Hill' addition was
easily understandable in view of the gentle rise of
the Cotswolds behind the village, and although
Tamara was quite familiar with the Cotswolds, this
particular village was new to her.

'Pub looks nice,' Nigel commented regretfully as
they drove through the village and turned left over
an ancient hump-backed bridge barely wide
enough for the car.

'Is it much farther?' Tamara asked him curiously.

'Three or four miles. Interesting chap, our host,'
he added thoughtfully. 'I'd never have put him
down as the philanthropic type—he's a damned
sight too hard and shrewd. Could have knocked
me down with a feather when he told me that he
intended to use the royalties from his book to equip
and run his home as a rehabilitation centre. Of
course he'll still have the land, and there's a sizeable
dower house, apparently, but even so . . .'

'What's he like?' Tamara asked, her curiosity
stirring. For some reason she pictured a peppery
gentleman in his sixties, rather dapper, and charm-
ing in a way that deceived no one as to his true
character.

'Wait and see,' Nigel replied mysteriously. 'What
did you think of the outline?' He had given it to her
to read earlier in the week.

'Very impressive,' she agreed. 'Almost frightening if it wasn't a blend of fact and fiction.'

'I'm not so sure it is,' Nigel astounded her by
saying. 'In fact I have a strong suspicion that our

author is using more fact than fiction, but is carefully disguising it to lessen the blow.'

The outline Tamara had read concerned a dangerous leakage from a Winscale-type plant, and the authorities' determined suppression of that fact, and the frightening results of the suppression. Tamara had found what she had read chillingly frightening, and she looked a little uncertainly at Nigel, asking him.

'But how could it possibly be true?'

'I don't know. But I do know that he has contacts pretty high up in the Army and he may have got the initial whisper from them. Ah, this looks like it,' he commented as iron gates suddenly loomed up at the side of the road.

The small lodge seemed to be deserted, so Tamara had to climb out of the car to open the gates. The drive was choked with weeds, and the grounds a wilderness of rhododendrons and azaleas.

'It must have been lovely once,' she commented as she caught a glimpse of a small lake, choked with weed, and then the drive forked abruptly, causing Nigel to frown slightly over his instructions.

'The right fork is the one we take,' he told Tamara. 'The main house isn't being used at the moment—something about problems with the roof, so we want the Dower House.'

They found it round a long curve in the drive, and Tamara caught her breath in delight when she saw the perfect Regency house with its graceful shape and symmetry, the warm brick dyed rose-gold by the sun.

Nigel aparked his BMW next to the elegant Porsche. Obviously Nigel's new find wasn't exactly short of money, Tamara reflected as she followed her boss up the shallow flight of steps.

A middle-aged man of soldierly bearing opened the door to them and they stepped into a rectangular hall with a beautiful double staircase curving up to an overhanging gallery. Tamara had a brief impression of white and gold décor, and the magnificence of a Waterford chandelier, and Adam decor, and then one of the doors leading off the hall opened and everything else faded from her mind as she stood rooted to the spot, every shred of colour fading from her face, leaving it as matt white as the beautifully painted walls.

'Zach!' Nigel was striding forward, his hand extended, unaware of Tamara's frozen stance. 'Great to see you. Can I introduce my assistant to you? Tamara, come and meet our new author-to-be.'

Somehow she found herself moving forward, as mechanically as a jointed doll, her lips stiff with the effort of maintaining the rigid smile she had pinned to them, a cold clamminess invading her body, her eyes unable to meet the cold green ones she remembered so well.

'Tamara and I have already met,' Zach murmured expressionlessly. 'In the Caribbean and then again more recently. She's engaged to a neighbour of mine. Tell me,' he invited, turning to Tamara, 'have I managed to convince your fiancé yet that I have no intention of allowing them to hunt over my land?'

Tamara made a suitably noncommittal reply, glad of the shadows in the hall to conceal her flushed expression. She could feel Nigel watching her with sudden speculation, and all her fears crystallised when she heard him saying to Zach,

'You met in the Caribbean, you say? Quite a coincidence. Did you enjoy your holiday?'

'It had its moments.'

Tamara dared not look at either of them. She bitterly regretted confiding in Nigel to the extent of telling him that she had fallen in love with someone she had met on holiday. He was far too astute not to guess the truth, but surely he wouldn't betray her?

She held her breath when Zach said to Nigel, 'I understand you'll soon have to look for a new secretary?'

'Er . . .' For a moment Nigel looked perplexed and then he said cheerfully, 'Oh, you mean when she gets married? Oh, she'll be with me for quite a while yet, no firm date has been set—has it, Tamara?'

'No,' Tamara agreed huskily.

'Lunch is ready, Colonel.'

Colonel! Tamara's eyes swung to Zach's impenetrable face. That was something he hadn't told her during their imprisonment together. When she had talked about being in charge she had assumed he meant as a Captain or a Major.

'Johnson tends to forget that I've left the Army,' Zach explained dryly as the manservant disappeared silently. 'He was under my command and invalided out, but the old habits die hard.'

Tamara's mind whirled. Zach had told her that he had to prove that he was no longer afraid of the jungle and she had assumed he meant because of his career, but now it seemed that he was no longer in the Army, and yet he had proved beyond a shadow of doubt that he had overcome the devils haunting him.

'Colonel, eh?' Nigel murmured as they followed

Zach into a pleasantly furnished dining room. Most of the furniture was antique, but it possessed none of the heaviness of Malcolm's parents' antiques. The dining room overlooked lawned gardens to the rear of the house, and some attempt had obviously been made to clear the flower beds of the choking weeds. Stately trees framed the rear of the garden, an attractive terrace apparently running the width of the back of the house, its stone balustrade weathered with age.

Johnson returned to pour them sherry, his manner stiff and very correct. He would shield Zach like a guard dog, Tamara sensed, and woe betide anyone who crossed him.

'Mrs Wilkes is ready to serve lunch now, Colonel,' he informed Zach woodenly, before departing.

'I think Johnson is trying to tell me that if we don't sit down there'll be hysterics in the kitchen,' Zach commented humorously. 'Actually I'm very fortunate in having both Johnson and Mrs Wilkes, although they to tend to be rather like oil and water. Johnson, you see, is a confirmed woman-hater, while Mrs Wilkes is, I suspect, looking for a second husband. However, she's an excellent cook. I saw your fiancé the other day,' he commented to Tamara without changing his tone of voice. 'He was out riding with a rather attractive brunette—Karen, I believe he called her.'

'Yes, that would be Karen Anstruther,' Tamara replied with commendable composure, refusing to rise to what she knew to be a deliberate taunt. 'She's Malcolm's secretary and her parents are close neighbours of his.'

'How cosy!'

Fortunately the arrival of iced melon wedges provided a welcome interruption, and Tamara concentrated on the delicious fruit while Nigel skilfully drew Zach out about his novel.

As a bystander Tamara was amused to see how well Zach parried Nigel's more searching questions, but underneath her amusement lay a pain that shadowed her eyes and brought a hard tight lump of tears to her throat.

Their main course consisted of spare ribs and a delicious assortment of garden-fresh vegetables.

'I'm afraid it's only cheese and biscuits for dessert,' Zach apologised smoothly when Mrs Wilkes had removed their plates. 'When Nigel told me he wanted to bring his assistant for some reason I expected a man.'

'No way,' Nigel chuckled. 'For one thing no man could possibly be as decorative, but as it happens, Tamara is the best secretary I've ever had. How long do you think it will take to get the first chapters done?' he asked Zach. 'I'd like to try and bring the book out in time for next year's Christmas trade, but that will mean a bit of a rush. I'm off to Milan next week—I've got a book lined up there. Someone who claims to be in the know about the Italian terrorists—says they've got some pretty high-up Government connections. Probably a load of waffle, but one can't afford not to investigate.'

'How long do you expect to be away?' Zach enquired politely.

'Er . . . two or three weeks, it just depends. Now, about your novel, how long do you think before you can let me have those early chapters?'

It was plain to Tamara that Nigel was anxious to pin Zach down to a definite contract, and having read what he had done Tamara could understand why.

'I could probably let you have the first three by the time you get back,' Zach replied smoothly, 'provided you're willing to loan me the services of your assistant.'

There was a sharp clatter as Tamara's knife fell from nerveless fingers, and then Nigel was saying quickly,

'Of course I'll find you a secretary, Zach, there's plenty of girls in the office who'd be delighted to . . .'

And just as quickly and far more determinedly Zach was interrupting blandly, 'That's very kind of you, Nigel, but I prefer to work with someone I know if possible, and Tamara can't possibly come with any better recommendation than your own. As you said yourself, you'll be away, and of course I don't expect to use her . . . skill for free.'

Had Nigel noticed the insulting way in which Zach had lingered over those last few words? Tamara wondered, not able to look at either of them.

She knew Nigel must have guessed that Zach was the father of her baby and he had tried to circumvent Zach's suggestion tactfully.

'It's up to you,' Zach added with a nicely judged touch of boredom. 'If you want the chapters . . .'

'Of course, of course,' Nigel agreed quickly. 'Would you mind, Tamara?'

'I . . . I don't see how I could do it,' she said huskily, 'I couldn't possibly commute.' Too late she realised that Zach would probably expect her to stay with Malcolm's parents too, but to her dismay he shrugged and said coolly,

'Of course not, but that's no problem. There's

half a dozen bedrooms lying empty here, and in point of fact it would probably be more convenient to have you on the premises. I take it that if it's necessary you won't mind working some evenings? I'll make it worth your while, of course.'

With what? Tamara longed to scream at him, hating the insulting way he looked and spoke, but for Nigel's sake she suppressed the words and merely replied tonelessly, 'If it means the work can be completed more quickly that will be all the payment I'll need.'

She had the satisfaction of seeing Zach's skin darken slightly under his tan, but when he turned aside to say something to Nigel, a wave of nausea suddenly swept her, forcing her to her feet, her lips as pale as her skin as she swayed sickly.

'Tamara!' Nigel was at her side instantly. Tamara forced a small smile.

'I'm fine,' she lied. 'If I could just go outside for a moment—some fresh air.'

'Of course.' Imperturbably Zach led the way to the french windows, opening them and allowing her to precede him outside. Tamara had grown used to feeling queasy first thing in the morning, but this was the first time she had felt so desperately ill during the day. She longed to creep away somewhere and be on her own. To her relief Nigel, sensitive to her distress, drew Zach's attention to something inside the dining room, and Tamara walked the length of the balustraded terrace, taking deep calming breaths of the pure fresh air. She was just about to venture across the smooth expanse of the lawn when her earlier nausea returned, leaving her retching helplessly, her face pressed to the cool brickwork, while her body shuddered agonisingly.

'So . . . An old trick but an effective one. I doubt

the Colonel will wish his grandson to be born out of wedlock. But why?'

Zachary was leaning against the balustrade, surveying her wan face with an intensity of anger that almost frightened her.

'Why what?' she stammered.

'Why get yourself pregnant?' Zach demanded brusquely. 'And don't tell me you're not. Mrs Wilkes would be mortified if she thought that was the effect her cooking had on my guests, but it wasn't the cooking, was it, Tamara? So I'll ask you again—why? Frightened you might lose him to Karen after all?'

'It's none of your damned business!' Tamara cried, goaded beyond endurance, almost hating him for suggesting that she had actually planned to become pregnant to force Malcolm to marry her. It was on the tip of her tongue to tell him that her engagement was over, but if he should then guess the truth and suspect her of engineering him into marriage instead of Malcolm. No, she could not bear that!

'No?' There was silky menace in the word. 'You won't forget that while you're here living under my roof, you're here to work for me, not spend your time with Mellor?'

'Malcolm is in New York at present,' Tamara told him curtly.

'Is he indeed? Does he know yet, or are you keeping it a happy secret until he comes back? You won't be able to wait much longer, will you?' he asked insultingly. 'What's it going to be? A seven months prem?'

Tamara's fingers curled impotently into her palms, itching to wipe the sardonic look off the autocratic male face above her.

'Tamara, are you okay?'

Nigel appeared on the terrace, his forehead creased in a frown. 'While we're here, Zach, how about showing us over the main house, and telling us a bit about your plans for it?'

At first Tamara thought he was going to refuse, but then he seemed to change his mind.

'What gave you the idea in the first place?' Nigel asked him as they walked through the garden to the drive which apparently led to the main house.

'Oh, it grew on me gradually. I inherited this place from an uncle—quite out of the blue. The main house had been neglected for years. The old man had offered it to the National Trust and they'd refused—they won't take any house without at least some sort of contribution towards its upkeep, but Gerald wouldn't accept this, and so to punish them he started to let the house collapse around his ears.

'Fortunately for me the Dower House was tenanted and the tenants kept it in good order.

'As for turning the main house into a rehabilitation centre—I suppose the germ of the idea was born when I did a tour in Northern Ireland. Those kids don't stand a chance; from the very moment of their birth hatred of the opposing religion is inculcated into them; they drink it in with their mother's milk, and it's much the same over here with the children who eventually become petty criminals and victims of racial violence. What I want to do is to give them a chance—before it's too late—to discover an alternative way of life, to live not in some approved school or remedial centre but in a place that teaches them self-respect and self-reliance . . .' He broke off suddenly. 'Sorry about that, I tend to let myself get carried away once I start.'

'Don't apologise,' Nigel smiled at him. 'I admire you—and envy you in a way, and I wish you every success.'

'I'll need it,' Zach replied grimly, 'and my first success must be my book.'

'I can see why,' Nigel agreed frankly as they rounded the final bend and the house stood before them, decaying and dismal; a hotch-potch of styles and tastes. Tiles were missing from the roof; windows broken; the whole place had a tired, defeated air that touched Tamara's heart.

'What made you go into the Army?' he asked suddenly. 'You were at Cambridge, weren't you?'

'Yes. In those days I planned to be a writer, but somehow I found myself becoming more and more disenchanted with the privileged world I inhabited. I left Cambridge without my degree and bummed around the world for a couple of years. I got involved with a group of mercenaries in Africa and discovered I had a talent for commanding men. It seemed only sensible if I was going to fight to do so with the best, so I came home and joined the Army.'

Having already learned the skills which must have made him invaluable to the S.A.S., Tamara thought inwardly, suspecting that Nigel had no idea of what Zach's role in the Army had actually been.

Zach showed them over the huge rambling house, pointing out its possibilities. There was a home farm attached to the estate, on which the boys would work.

'We can't be entirely self-supporting, of course,' he admitted, 'but the farm runs profitably and there's still scope for the small specialised engineering units of a type we could set up here. I've several ideas in mind.'

It was late afternoon before Nigel and Tamara left. They drove several miles in silence, and then Nigel said softly,

'That's him, isn't it? The man you fell in love with; the father of your child?'

'Was I so obvious?' Tamara asked wryly.

'No. I was just putting two and two together. I'm sorry about landing you with the job of helping him with his book.'

'There wasn't any way you could get out of it,' Tamara admitted wearily. 'He thinks I'm still engaged to Malcolm—I didn't tell him the truth because . . .'

'Because you don't want him to guess that the baby is his?' Nigel supplied gently. 'He seemed very insistent on having you work for him.'

'Punishment,' Tamara explained briefly. 'He seems to think I'm forcing Malcolm into a marriage that he doesn't want. He even accused me of becoming pregnant to force Malcolm's hand.'

There was a shocked silence and then Nigel said worriedly, 'Tamara, if you don't feel that you can cope with this. You've got the baby to worry about now, as well you know. If you feel he's going to give you a hard time . . .'

'The boot ought to be on the other foot,' Tamara joked lightly. 'How times change! It used to be the woman who hated and despised her vile seducer, and now . . . now . . .'

A soft white hankie was pushed into her trembling hands. Nigel let her cry for a few minutes and then when she had herself under control and had blown her small nose defiantly, he said, 'Tamara, are you sure about this, I could tell him you've changed your mind?'

And have him find out later from Malcolm that

their engagement was over and had been for some weeks, and then possibly guess the truth?

'No,' she said firmly. 'It's probably the best thing that could have happened to me. Living in such close proximity to him is bound to . . .'

'Change the way you feel about him?' Nigel suggested, shaking his head. 'I don't think you honestly believe that, do you, Tam?'

'Stranger things have been known to happen.'

But she knew that Nigel was right and that living in the same house as Zach was more likely to deepen her love than wither it. If contempt and dislike had not killed it, what possible chance had a tepid thing like familiarity?

CHAPTER NINE

'THIS will be your room—it has its own bathroom, and the Colonel is just down the corridor.'

Johnson was showing Tamara to her bedroom. He had greeted her on her arrival at the house with the information that Zach had gone into Gloucester on business but that he would return shortly.

The bedroom he showed her to was comfortably furnished with delicate French Empire furniture and a soft pearl grey carpet. The bathroom off it repeated the grey and pink colour scheme of the bedroom, and although the decor and soft furnishings had a faintly old-fashioned air, it was plain that they were of excellent quality.

Tamara suspected that the tenants had been an older couple, and this was borne out by Mrs Wilkes when she brought her a tray of tea ten minutes later.

'I don't normally come in unless the Colonel is having guests for dinner, but he asked me special like, seeing as this is your first day.'

And Mrs Wilkes had jumped at the chance of discovering what the newcomer was like, Tamara guessed, smiling her thanks.

'So you're going to help the Colonel with his book,' she pronounced, plainly reluctant to leave before her curiosity had been satisfied. 'All agog, everyone round here was when he inherited the estate. Plans to turn the old house into a centre for wayward boys. That won't go down too well with some, but then live and let live, that's what I always say,' she added virtuously, her arms folded over her ample form. 'Think you'll like it down here, do you? The Colonel's a fine-looking man,' she added.

'This tea is delicious, Mrs Wilkes,' Tamara praised, sidestepping the questions. 'Just what I needed, but you mustn't spoil me like this . . .'

'Oh, the Colonel's asked me to come in every day while you're here, miss,' the housekeeper surprised Tamara by saying. 'Says you'll be too busy to stop and prepare meals,' she added. 'Seems like you'll be working morning, noon and night.'

'My firm is anxious to get the Colonel's book into production,' Tamara explained briefly, 'and as my boss is away at the moment I'm here to help where I can.'

'Brought your own typewriter with you, so Johnson says.'

'Yes, it's upstairs in my room.'

'I doubt you'll need it. The Colonel's had a fine new electric machine installed in the library for you.'

Zachary arrived while Tamara was still unpacking. She had brought with her the new clothes she had bought for work—trim suits, neat skirts and blouses. Although many of the girls wore jeans for work, she could still not bring herself to totally throw off the habits instilled by Aunt Lilian, and the thought of wearing anything as casual as jeans for work was not her style. She had brought a pair with her, though—tossed into her case at the last minute in case she got the opportunity to explore the grounds. Zach had talked about working in the evening, but surely he didn't intend to work every evening?

Tamara acknowledged that she was deliberately dawdling over the last of her unpacking because she was reluctant to face him, but at last the moment could be put off no longer. She paused, staring at her reflection in the mirror. As yet there was no hint of her pregnancy in her wand-slim body—if anything she had lost weight—but there was a new glossiness to her hair, a subtle rounding of her face and luminescence to her complexion.

Her outfit was another of her new ones, a pale blue skirt with a elasticated waist, and buttons down the front. With it she was wearing a white tee-shirt with a pretty blue butterfly motif. The outfit had been bought from a High Street chain store, but it looked attractive and fresh and was a world away from the dull repressed clothes she had chosen before she met Zach.

Unaware of the fragile vulnerability of her face, she went downstairs head held high, ready to face her tormentor.

Johnson was in the hall and he directed her to the library-cum-study. Tamara knocked and walked in. For a long moment there was complete silence while Zachary studied her slender body, and then with several lithe strides he was at her side, pulling from her hair the pins with which she had secured it on a last-minute impulse.

'Never let me see you with your hair screwed up like that again,' he demanded sharply. 'I may not be your fiancé, with all the privileges that the word implies, but I'll be damned if I'm going to sit opposite you day after day with your hair forced into a bun like a schoolmarm!'

'It's tidier like that,' Tamara lied evenly, despising herself for the hurried jump her heart had given at his reference to her hair.

'Maybe so, but don't be tempted to wear it like that again, otherwise I might just show you how untidy it could be. Come here, I want to show you something.'

For a moment his abrupt change of front startled her, but when he frowned she hurried to his side, staring in some dismay at the keyboard and V.D.U. unit arranged on a low desk.

'The latest word processor,' he told her, bending over the machine, to switch it on. 'Let me show you how it works.'

Forced into such close proximity, Tamara could smell the clean fragrance of his cologne, her senses responding immediately to the heat she could feel coming off his body. He was dressed casually in jeans and a checked shirt, stretched across the hard muscles of his back, the sunlight streaming in through the window dancing on the polished bones of his face.

'Something wrong?'

She tore her eyes away from the sensuously full curve of his lower lip, her heart racing like a trip hammer.

'N-nothing.'

'Good. Now, watch this.' He gave her a brief demonstration of how to work the processor. 'It's very similar to a normal electric keyboard really, but this way we save time in the long run, because the processor can store everything you type and then when we want to alter something we can call it back and simply change whatever is necessary.'

'And then the machine produces a perfectly typed altered copy,' Tamara concluded.

'You have had some experience of them, then?'

'Yes, we have one at the office.'

'Good,' Zach said crisply. 'That means we won't

have to waste time on you getting used to it. What I propose is that I dictate to you in the morning, and then leave you free to type in the afternoons. I'll then check what you've done and if any alterations are necessary we'll do them that evening. When is Mellors due back from New York?' he added abruptly.

Tamara hadn't the faintest idea, and lied vaguely, 'I'm really not sure. It all depends on how fast he can complete his business.'

'Does he know about your condition yet?'

Tamara lifted her chin.

'Don't you think that's our business?' she asked sweetly. 'I'm here to work for you—that doesn't entitle you to ask questions about my personal life.'

'It does entitle me to ensure that I get value for money,' Zach countered cruelly. 'I don't want you mooning all over the place because you're missing your lover. It's counter-productive.'

'So what are you suggesting?' Tamara stormed back, completely forgetting the danger. 'That you take his place? You couldn't.'

'You're right,' Zach agreed curtly. 'I wouldn't have the stomach for it.'

It was only the shrill ring of the telephone that prevented Tamara from announcing there and then that she was leaving.

Zach picked up the receiver, his hard face relaxing into an amused smile as he listened.

'I've missed you too, Julie,' Tamara heard him say. She made to leave, but he waved her into a chair, his eyes on her face, his smile deepening as he listened intently to whoever was on the other end of the line.

'No, I'm sorry, I can't possibly come up to

London at the moment. Look, why don't you come down here?'

Tamara heard him laugh, and then he turned away from her and out of politeness she stared stolidly through the window, deliberately blotting out the sound of his voice, all the time wondering who this Julie was who could make him smile so easily.

'Sorry about that,' he apologised insincerely, when he had replaced the receiver. 'An old friend. She's coming down to spend a few days with me. Now where was I? Ah, yes, the word processor . . . Well, if you think you feel confident about using it I suggest you go and rest before dinner.' A sneer curled his mouth. 'In your condition you can't afford to overdo things, can you?'

In the end Tamara pleaded tiredness and sent a message with Johnson excusing herself from dinner. To her surprise Mrs Wilkes arrived with a tempting tray half an hour later, her forehead creased with concern.

'The Colonel says you're not feeling too well. All that driving from London, I expect, takes it out of you. I've brought you a nice omelette and a pot of tea.'

Tamara thanked her, her guilt increasing when she thought of the extra work her cowardice had caused. It was true that the drive down had been tiring. It was a long time since she had driven so far and her small Mini was not built for long journeys. She would have to change it once the baby arrived. She fell into a daydream about the baby, her omelette growing cold on the plate.

Zach had not specified what time he wanted her to start work in the morning, but Tamara was downstairs at eight, estimating that this would give her time to have her breakfast and present herself in the library for nine.

Mrs Wilkes looked shocked when she insisted that all she wanted was toast and coffee.

'Bad as the Colonel,' she grumbled. 'Although at least he had some scrambled eggs.'

'The Colonel's had his breakfast, then, has he?' Tamara questioned, feeling both relief and dismay. She didn't want to get off on the wrong foot on her first day. Despite her personal feelings towards Zach, she was determined to remain as professional towards him as she could, and she prided herself on her efficiency as a secretary.

'Oh yes,' Mrs Wilkes confirmed. 'Always has his breakfast at six-thirty, does the Colonel. Habit he got into in the Army, apparently. Johnson makes it for him. By the way,' she added, 'he asked me to tell you to go along to the library when you're ready. Always goes for a walk about breakfast, he does, rain or shine, but he'll be back by now.'

It was ten to nine when Tamara knocked on the library door and walked in. Zach was sitting behind the large desk, studying some papers. He looked up when Tamara walked in.

'Good morning,' she said formally, smoothing her navy skirt with nervous fingers, feeling selfconsciously formal when faced with Zach's lean, jeans-clad figure. He got up and walked round the desk to come and stand in front of her.

'Quite the perfect secretary, aren't we?' he jeered. 'But I'm glad you remembered about the hair.'

'If you're ready to begin,' Tamara said quietly, ignoring his taunts.

Two hours later, her fingers cramped from

taking shorthand, she gave a mental sigh of relief when Mrs Wilkes appeared with a tray of coffee.

'No sugar for me,' Zach said laconically, indicating that Tamara should pour. 'Would you like to break for half an hour? I don't want to overtire you.'

His last words made her temper flare. She was tired, her body stiff, but she was damned if she would let him see it.

'That's hardly likely,' she said crisply. 'By all means let's continue while the book's flowing. That way we'll finish all the sooner.'

For some obscure reason her words seemed to annoy him, and Tamara had increasing difficulty keeping up with his dictation during the second half of the morning; one half of her mind concentrating on what he was saying while the other marvelled at his ability to work without checking or hesitating.

'I think we've got the bones of the first chapter there,' he announced just after half past twelve. 'Lunch is at one. How long do you think it will take you to type that lot back?'

Judging by the number of pages of shorthand in her book, Tamara estimated that it would take her all afternoon and the best part of the evening as well.

'I'm not sure,' she said icily, 'but I won't stop until it's done.'

It was a vow she was to regret as the afternoon wore on and the ache low down in her back grew steadily worse, as her fingers flew over the keys, her forehead creased in concentration.

'Not still at it, are you?' Mrs Wilkes exclaimed in disapproval at six o'clock when she came in to remove the afternoon tea tray.

Tamara used the interruption to check on the number of pages still to type, her heart sinking as she realised she was barely halfway through.

'I'll have to give dinner a miss tonight, Mrs Wilkes,' she apologised. 'Would it be asking too much for me to have a glass of milk and some fruit instead?'

'Not as far as I'm concerned,' Mrs Wilkes told her, adding roundly, 'But if you ask me, you're asking too much of your body, working all through the day and half the night besides with nothing inside you.'

Zach had gone out. Tamara had heard the car, and besides, he had told her he had to go in to Bath for some reference books he needed, and all the time she was working her ears were alert for sounds of his return.

At eight o'clock she flexed her stiff shoulders and paused to drink her milk, wondering where he was. Perhaps he'd gone to see some friends ... Julie perhaps ... Jealousy tore through her, followed by an irrational surge of anger that he should be out enjoying himself while she was exhausting her mind and body on his book.

It was just after eleven when she pulled the final page of typing out of the machine, too exhausted even to check it. Picking up her tray, she took it to the kitchen and then wearily climbed the stairs.

In her bedroom it was almost too much of an effort to undress, but her muscles were so stiff and tense that she felt she needed the luxurious warmth of a bath to help her relax.

She was just on the verge of falling asleep when she heard the Porsche returning. She had left the manuscript on Zach's desk—all forty-five pages of it—and smiled grimly with weary satisfaction, sure

that he had not expected her to finish it and that
he had dictated so much purely to punish her.

She was awake at six, her sleep disturbed by
unfamiliar sounds. Her straining ears caught footsteps disappearing in the direction of the stairs and
she glanced at her watch in weary disbelief, before
remembering Mrs Wilkes saying that Zach break-
fasted at six.

Well, let him, she thought crossly, punching her
pillow, but did that mean that everyone else had to
be woken at the same godforsaken hour?

It was with considerably less energy that she
went down for breakfast. Her back was still stiff,
her shoulder muscles aching with tension, a terrible
tiredness enveloping her.

'Decent food, that's what you need,' Mrs Wilkes
told her sharply when she saw her pale face. 'Beats
me how you young things think a body keeps on
going when you don't feed it properly!'

She tried to persuade Tamara into something
more substantial than toast and tea, but Tamara's
still delicate stomach revolted at the thought of
anything less bland.

At nine o'clock on the dot she presented herself in
the library, too weary to admire, as she had done the
previous day, the beautiful Aubusson carpet and the
fine veneered yew bookshelves that lined the walls.

Zach was standing by the window, frowning over
the typed pages in his hand.

'There are several mistakes in these last pages,'
he told her coldly. 'I've marked the other alterations I want to make. If you're ready I'll dictate
the new passages.'

His eyes, cold and impersonal, swept her trim
figure in a dark blue skirt and a soft voile blouse
in a pretty spotted fabric.

Tamara's fingers were aching by the time he had finished. A glance at her watch confirmed that it was nearly eleven o'clock—with the alterations and corrections he had pointed out it would be late afternoon before she had finished work.

'I've got to go and see a builder I've commissioned to work on the main house,' Zach told her when he had finished. 'I'll be over there for most of the afternoon.'

Perhaps she ought to be thankful for small mercies, Tamara reflected tiredly when he had gone; at least with Zach out of sight she would be able to concentrate on her work without constantly being distracted by his proximity and her body's treacherous reaction to it. Even when she was hating him for what he was doing to her, her body still melted yieldingly every time he came near her.

When Mrs Wilkes brought her a tray of tea at three o'clock she exclaimed over Tamara's wan face and strained eyes.

'Doing too much, that's what you are,' she told Tamara, 'and you mark my words, no good will come of it!'

She came in half an hour later, greatly perturbed, to tell Tamara that her eldest daughter who was expecting her second child had gone into labour a month earlier than expected.

'I'll have to go, because there's no one else to look after our Kevin—his dad's at work, and besides, I promised our Susan I'd mind him, but I don't like letting the Colonel down.'

'I'm sure he'll understand,' Tamara assured her. 'Don't worry, you just go.'

'I've made a casserole for dinner and there's nothing to do except the potatoes and veg . . .'

When she had gone Tamara stretched wearily.

She still had corrections to make and then she would have to process the new copy, but her back was aching so badly that she simply had to rest. She sat down in the comfortable leather chair—one of a pair either side of the fire—intending just to rest for ten minutes, but ten minutes stretched to twenty, her eyes closed, her breathing deepened and slowed.

Later, when the library door opened, she didn't stir, and Zach checked a swift exclamation, his mouth tightening as he saw the pale mauve shadows of exhaustion beneath her eyes.

'Looks like the lass has done too much,' Johnson commented lugubriously. 'And Mrs Wilkes isn't here either, although there's a casserole in the oven.'

'You go and organise some food, I'll take Miss Forbes upstairs,' Zach instructed him. 'There's no point in waking her up now.'

It was dark when Tamara finally awoke from her deep sleep. It was several seconds before she realised that she wasn't downstairs in the library but in bed, and that someone had undressed her.

A shadow moved by the door.

'So, you're awake. Are you hungry?'

She shook her head, sudenly dreadfully selfconscious as Zach detached himself from the wall and came towards her, her heart in her throat as he stood over her, piercing the darkness to find her pale face, as he waited for her to answer his question.

'No,' she told him huskily. 'I'm sorry I fell asleep . . . I don't seem to have as much energy since . . .' Her face flamed under the protective cover of the darkened room, and she bit her lip, faltering into silence, feeling the tension emanating from the male body above her.

'Damn you, Tamara,' Zach muttered thickly, bending suddenly to capture her parted mouth with the warmth of his, and desire spread to every part of her body from the heated possession of his kiss, his fingers burning into her skin as he drew her upwards and held her against his body. She could feel the suddenly urgent thud of his heart, and knew that her own copied it, her pulses racing unevenly as he moved his lips from her mouth to the soft curve of her jaw, and from there to the vulnerable hollows behind her ears. As his hand sought and found the rounded curve of her breast warning bells rang in Tamara's brain. She didn't know what had sparked off Zach's desire for her—but she did know that it spelled intense danger to her—danger that she might betray herself to him, and for that reason she resisted the magnetic pull of his personality, and stiffened in his arms, forcing her lips into a firm line as she said coolly,

'No, Zach. You seem to have forgotten, I'm engaged to Malcolm.'

She felt him tense, his eyes searching her face, boring into hers as though he intended to read all her most personal thoughts.

'Maybe I ought to remind you how easily you forget that fact before,' he said silkily. 'Or don't you think I can?'

When she didn't speak, he lowered his head, trailing tormenting kisses against her throat, his voice rough with arousal as he said huskily, 'Want me to prove it you?'

Her strangled 'No!' came a split second too late, and instead of stopping him, merely gave him access to the inner sweetness of her mouth, setting alight a thousand nerve endings as he delicately traced the shape of her mouth, the soft kisses he pressed upon it sending her into a mindless fever of desire. She moaned softly, her whole body trembling as she pressed her mouth to the skin exposed by the open neck of his shirt, all warnings forgotten as her fingers touched blindly over his body, his skin moist beneath her shaking mouth.

'Tamara!'

Her name was a muffled groan, her own protest smothered beneath the demanding pressure of his mouth. She never wanted the kiss to end; never wanted to let reality intrude on her perfect fairytale world where she could safely ignore the truth and pretend that Zachary felt for her what she felt for him.

She moaned in pleasure as he pushed aside her nightdress. 'Have you any idea what undressing you did to me?' he demanded hoarsely as his hand cupped her breast, his thumb stroking sensually over the already aroused peak. 'Have you any idea what just having you here in this house does to me? I might despise myself for wanting you, but I still do. It's like a sickness in my blood. God knows I loathe myself for it, but sometimes the sheer pleasure of giving in to one's weaker impulses overrides the cautious voice warning of the self-disgust to be endured later. This is one of those moments, Tamara ... and you want me too, for all that you're engaged to Mellors. Your body wants me,' he told her huskily.

Tamara was past responding coherently. Her hands locked behind his head, revelling in the silky feel of his dark hair, pleasure swelling in waves through her body as his mouth explored the shape of her breasts and the valley between them, his weight shifting to allow him to explore the trembling contours of her body.

'It doesn't feel any different,' he told her in a drugged voice, 'at least not outwardly. What's it like, knowing his child is growing inside you?' His mouth touched the vulnerable swell on her stomach and all Tamara's muscles contracted in ecstasy and pain. If only she could tell him the truth and say that it was his child, and that she delighted in the knowledge of its being there. But these were words that could never be spoken. In a moment of weakness he might want her as he did now, but Tamara was in no doubts as to his real feelings for her.

Her sensitive flesh quivered as Zach's mouth possessed each breast briefly before it returned to explore the sensitive curve of her throat, her own lips pressing feverishly hot kisses against his damp skin, her fingers tugging impatiently at his shirt buttons.

'Are you like this with Mellors?' Zach demanded hoarsely. 'Are you, Tamara—tell me!'

His words brought her back to reality, reminding her of the low opinion he had of her. Tears ached in her throat. A brief knock on the bedroom door stiffened her body, and Zach got up with a muffled curse.

'Telephone, Colonel,' Tamara heard Johnson call. 'It's Miss Julie.'

Julie! Tamara turned away from Zach, burying her face in the rumpled bedclothes, overcome with the pain of her own self-delusion.

'I see your fiancé's back.'

The words were like a splash of cold water, and Tamara stiffened in her chair. They were having lunch and these were the first personal words Zach had spoken to her since that night in her room. She was in no doubt that he regretted the incident and wanted to make it plain to her that it had been nothing more than an aberration brought on by physical desire for a woman—any woman!

'I saw him this morning,' Zach told her. 'He was out riding—with his secretary.'

Somehow Tamara managed to go on eating without betraying her shock, although the food tasted like sawdust and she felt she would never be able to swallow it.

'You didn't know, did you?' Zach goaded. 'It seems to me that he's nowhere near as keen to marry you as he ought to be. Never mind, you still hold the final trump card, don't you?'

'Miss Julie's arrived, Colonel.'

Not for the first time Tamara blessed Johnson's timely interruption. She had heard from Mrs Wilkes, whose daughter had given birth to another son, that Zach had asked her to prepare a room for his friend. It was a room several doors down from her own, and Tamara had been fiercely relieved to know it wasn't the one adjacent to Zach's, which Mrs Wilkes had told her was part of the master suite which Zach occupied. Not that that really meant anything. There was nothing to stop Julie sharing Zach's bed, or him hers.

When he went to welcome her, Tamara took herself off to the library. They had almost completed the third chapter. The book had come on extremely well, and after the earlier incident Zach had taken care to ensure that Tamara was not overworked.

She was checking some typing when he walked in, a vivacious redhead at his side, her smile faintly chilly as she surveyed Tamara.

'So this is what keeps you chained to the country!' she complained, her sapphire blue eyes hardening over Tamara's face.

'Yes,' Zach agreed blandly, 'my book. Nothing else would keep me away from you,' he assured her, sliding his arms round her waist and pulling her against him, before kissing her.

Tamara felt sick. She tried to concentrate on what she was doing, but all she could see was Zach's face, Zach's body, Zach's arms round another girl.

'Darling,' Julie purred when he eventually released her, 'that's what I call a welcome! I'm beginning to think you weren't fibbing after all when you said you missed me.'

'How long can you stay?' Zach heard him asking her as they left the room.

Tamara didn't hear the answer, but the next few days were sheer purgatory. It seemed that no matter where she went to escape from them, be it in the house or the grounds, she was fated to come across Zach and Julie, more often than not in one another's arms.

'T'ain't right,' Mrs Wilkes sniffed one morning, when she had been summoned upstairs and ordered to prepare a breakfast tray by Julie, who was still apparently in bed, although it was gone ten o'clock. 'Fancy piece with nothing to her but a flighty mind. The Colonel's a fool if he ties himself to that one.'

'He's a grown man, Mrs Wilkes,' Tamara reminded her in a hard voice. 'And now you really must excuse me, I want to try and get this chapter finished.'

As Mrs Wilkes confided to her daughter later, she knew when she wasn't wanted—and why!

On the third evening of Julie's visit Tamara excused herself from dinner. At breakfast the following morning she handed Zach the completed three chapters—perfectly produced by the word processor.

'If you don't mind I think I'll return to London this afternoon,' she told him calmly. 'After all, I've done the job I came to do . . .'

'Oh, but I do mind,' Zach said lightly. Julie was still in bed, and during her visit for some reason Zach had taken to delaying his breakfast until Tamara had hers. She daren't let herself think about the reasons for such a deviation from his routine, nor to wonder whether it had anything to do with the hours spent with Julie after she herself had gone to bed.

Tamara refused to respond to the goad. She had the feeling that he was deliberately baiting her, but she couldn't understand why. He had Julie now, so why continue to torment her?

'Nigel promised you to me for two to three weeks,' Zach reminded her.

'But we've finished the chapters.'

'We could do some more. Nigel would be delighted if we did.'

Tamara couldn't deny that.

'Why the rush to get away?' Zach asked her softly. 'I could feel mortally offended, especially when I've gone to the trouble of inviting your fiancé over here this morning.'

Tamara choked on her coffee, her face devoid of all colour. Malcolm here! She closed her eyes in anguish. Dear God, what was she going to do? The fabrication of her engagement wouldn't last a second in Zach's probing presence, and once that was gone he was fully capable of rending into shreds what was left of her pride and self-respect, to say nothing of discovering about his baby. Her hand went to her stomach.

'Thinking today might be a good time to tell him, with witnesses there to make sure he does the right thing?' Zach goaded, noticing the betraying gesture.

'I hate you!', Tamara burst out impulsively, pushing back her chair and rushing out of the room. 'I hate you!'

Upstairs she thought wildly of simply walking out and driving off in her car, but some inherent and stubborn streak of courage would not let her. If she was to be denounced and humiliated then let her at least have the guts to face up to it.

The morning dragged by. It was just after eleven when Tamara heard the sound of horses' hooves on the gravel drive. She was standing in the hall, almost rooted to the spot, two bright coins of colour burning in her cheeks, when Zach observed lazily,

'Well, aren't you going to go and say hello to him?'

Moving like a robot, Tamara walked towards the door. For a moment the sunlight dazzled her as she stepped outside and towards the drive.

'Tamara! Good God, what on earth are you doing here?'

Tamara looked upwards, shielding her eyes. Malcolm was riding the hunter he kept in his parents' stables and alongside him, looking very trim and supercilious, sat Karen Austruther on an obviously highly-strung thoroughbred mare.

Tamara, who liked horses but was faintly alarmed by them, stepped back instinctively, her eyes widening in sudden fear as Karen's horse

suddenly reared, pawing the air, the sharp whistle
of her crop as it sliced through the air and across
the animal's flanks bringing it forward in a furious
bound, its eyes rolling threateningly.

What happened next was a confused blur to
Tamara afterwards. One moment she was a safe
distance away from the horses, trying to think of
how she was going to explain her presence to
Malcolm, without betraying to Zach that their
engagement was over, the next, she was staring
upwards in terror while Karen's horse reared over
her, its hooves glinting in the sunshine as it came
down over her, slowly ... slowly ... and she was
unable to move.

'Mellors!' It was Zach's voice, furious and
authoritative, that broke the paralysing spell; his
arms that snatched her from danger to deposit her,
trembling uncontrollably, a safe distance away
from the prancing animal.

'For God's sake, man,' she heard Zachary saying
angrily, 'why the hell didn't you do something? She
could have been killed!'

Karen's acid laughter filtered into the morning
air. 'Don't be ridiculous! She wasn't in any real
danger. She ought to have moved out of the way.
She doesn't begin to know the first thing about
horses, that's all.'

They all stopped talking as a car suddenly came
down the drive. On a wave of relief Tamara recognised Nigel's BMW and started to hurry unsteadily
towards it as it came to a halt and Nigel climbed
out.

'Tamara, my dear girl. ... I wrapped up the
Italian business sooner than I anticipated and
decided to come and see how things were going
here.'

'She's just had an unpleasant shock,' Zach explained quietly. 'I believe you were just about to leave,' he added implacably to Malcolm and Karen.

'But I wanted to talk to you about the hunt,' Malcolm blustered. 'See here ... I think it's time you began to see reason. There are people living round here who don't care much for the idea of having a gang of young hooligans about the place ...'

'Yes,' Karen piped up in shrill tones. 'My father is a J.P. and he doesn't approve at all. It's just not the done thing round here, I can assure you.'

'No?' It seemed to Tamara that Zach's voice was dangerously quiet, and she shivered within the protection of Nigel's supporting arm. 'Well I can assure you, Miss ... whatever your name is, that there *are* people round here who have a damned sight more compassion for their fellow human beings than you appear to have, and they have a hell of a lot more pull than your father.'

Karen wheeled her horse round and cantered down the drive, Malcolm following her.

'Do you honestly think you can be happy with that life; with those narrow-minded views?' Zach demanded harshly of Tamara as he drew level with her. 'Because I damned well don't!'

She couldn't look at him. She turned to Nigel and said painfully, 'I want to go home. Please can we?'

CHAPTER TEN

'It's going to be fantastic,' Nigel exclaimed with a satisfied sigh as he replaced the final sheet of typescript. He had been reading the first three chapters of Zach's novel, and although it was only a week since Tamara had returned to London, her part in the preparation of the typescript seemed to belong to another lifetime.

She felt she could never do enough to show Nigel how grateful she was for his prompt action on that final, dreadful day of her stay with Zach. Competently and cheerfully he had whisked her away from the scene of her humiliation without giving either Zach or Malcolm any opportunity to question her.

'You're looking better,' he approved when he had finished reading. 'How are you feeling?'

'Fine,' Tamara assured him. She was beginning to get over the early morning nausea which had made her life such a misery in the first weeks of her pregnancy and although as yet there was scant outward alteration to her body, inwardly she was aware of the baby's growth, and the knowledge filled her with a warm inner glow. She caught sight of a newspaper on Nigel's desk and her colour faded a little as she saw the photograph of Zach and Julie, and the caption beneath it.

'Zach's plans for his house are beginning to catch the attention of the Press,' Nigel commented. 'Have you heard anything from him since you left?'

'Ought I to have done?' Tamara parried lightly.

There was pity and something else—admiration perhaps—in Nigel's eyes as they surveyed her downbent head.

'Not really, I suppose, but I thought he might have wanted to thank you for the excellent work you put in on his manuscript. It can't have been easy, rushing it through so quickly.'

'It wasn't,' Tamara agreed, thinking of the afternoon she had fallen into an exhausted sleep over her work and how she had woken up to find Zach in her room.

About Zach himself she tried hard not to think, but it wasn't always easy. Sometimes the memory of him would sneak up on her unawares, her mind forming a mental image of him and superimposing it on whatever she was doing.

Later in the afternoon the phone rang. Tamara picked up the receiver absently, then shock jolted through her as she recognised Zach's voice as he asked to be put through to Nigel.

The conversation lasted a good twenty minutes, and when it was over Nigel came into her office, raking fingers through his hair, his expression perturbed enough to make her heart thud erratically.

'Anything wrong?' she queried. 'He hasn't changed his mind about the book, has he?'

'No, nothing like that. He wants you to go back and work for him,' Nigel told her baldly. 'Oh, it's all right,' he assured her when he saw the consternation in her eyes. 'I told him it wasn't on; that I was too busy to manage without you.' He wasn't going to add to Tamara's worries by telling her that Zach had more or less held him to ransom over the completion of the manuscript on time if he refused to send Tamara down to work for him. 'Apparently he's got some bee in his bonnet about no other secretary being able to produce work of the same high standard as yours. You know how difficult some authors can be,' Nigel reminded her ruefully, speaking from personal experience. 'If everything isn't exactly to their liking they can't work.'

What was more to the point was probably that Zach had been unable to find someone he could browbeat into working as hard as she had done, Tamara thought irately; or someone he could derive so much pleasure from taunting. She had noticed that quite often after he had been particularly savage with her his output of work almost doubled; something to do with a sudden extra flow of adrenalin into the bloodstream, perhaps.

'Don't worry,' Nigel comforted her a second time. 'I've told him there's just no way I can spare you to work for him right now. I even offered to try and find him a replacement, so you'd better get on to some of the agencies and see what they can come up with. I know it's none of my business, but are you sure he's indifferent to you, Tamara? Bearing in mind what you told me it seems strange that he should want you working for him.'

'He enjoys tormenting me,' Tamara said bitterly. 'I suppose it's his way of punishing me, because wanting me made him aware of a weakness in himself and he despises weakness.'

'Mmm. Well, I don't suppose we'll hear anything more about it now. Get James Deacon on the phone for me, will you, I want to talk to him about the dust jacket for the new Brian Balfour.'

London was sweltering under a minor heatwave. It had begun just after Tamara returned to London, and so far had lasted five days. Listening to the weather forecast as she dressed, Tamara heard that the weather was likely to break during the day with violent thunderstorms late in the afternoon.

Outside in the street, the heavy oppression and sultry heat reminded her sharply of St Stephen's. Because of the heat she was dressed more casually than usual in a thin tee-shirt that moulded the slightly fuller curves of her breasts and hugged her narrow waist, and a toning button-through skirt made of comfortable heat-resisting cotton.

Nigel gave her an admiring smile when she walked into his office. 'You look cool and fresh,' he exclaimed enviously. In contrast he was dressed in a formal although lightweight suit, its jacket discarded to lie haphazardly on top of the filing cabinets, his tie loose and the top button of his shirt unfastened.

'I've got a board meeting at ten,' he told Tamara, 'but it shouldn't take more than an hour.'

With Nigel out the office was relatively quiet. Tamara dealt briskly and efficiently with the half dozen telephone calls she received, and then remembered the letter the postman had handed her as she stepped out of the flat that morning.

The handwriting, on expensive cream notepaper, was unfamiliar. She studied it for a moment before opening the envelope.

The letter was from Dot Partington, and guilt smote Tamara as she remembered promising faithfully to keep in touch with her. The letter was long and chatty, bringing the older woman vividly to mind. To make reparation for her earlier forgetfulness, Tamara extracted some of the notepaper she kept in her desk and started to write back.

In her letter Dot had asked if Tamara and Malcolm had yet set a date for their wedding. Rather than lie, Tamara wrote back that her engagement was off, without specifying why, explaining that she had given Malcolm his ring back on her return from holiday.

The letter was finished long before Nigel returned from his meeting, which had gone on longer than anticipated. When he walked in he was frowning.

'Something wrong?' Tamara queried, knowing that he liked using her as a sounding board for his frustration when the caution of the other board members got too much for him.

'Not really. Get Zach Fletcher on the phone for me, will you?'

Tamara knew better than to question him further when he was wearing that particular preoccupied look. She dialled Zach's number with shaking fingers, her stomach churning sickly while she waited for someone to answer.

Instinctively she had been bracing herself against hearing Zach answer, and hearing Julie's clear high voice instead was like a shock of icy water. She stammered a little over Zach's name and almost forgot to explain why she was calling, the omission bringing a chagrined flush to her too pale face, which she was thankful Zach was not there to see. The moment she heard his curt, 'Fletcher,' she put the call through to Nigel without speaking. The red light at the base of her phone which indicated that Nigel was still talking seemed to be on for a very long time. Another author arrived for an appointment and when he had been waiting for over ten minutes, Tamara did what she usually did in such circumstances, which was simply to scribble down a message informing Nigel that his appointment had arrived, and walk quietly into his office to place it on his blotter. As she opened the door and walked in she heard Nigel saying bitterly,

'Look, I take your point, Zach, but I don't like the way you went over my head. I told you I couldn't spare Tamara and I meant it. Now I've just had half the Board hauling me over the coals this morning for being obstructive.' He looked up, saw Tamara's white face, and said quickly into the receiver, 'Look, I must go now, I'll speak with you again,' and then he hung up.

'Was that true?' Tamara demanded through dry lips, the original purpose of her intrusion forgotton. 'Was that why you had to go to that meeting this morning? Because you told Zach I couldn't work for him?'

'It was one of the reasons, yes,' Nigel acknowledged. 'I've let the M.D. read the early chapters and he's wildly enthusiastic—so enthusiastic in fact that he's giving Zach the complete kid glove treatment.'

'You mean . . .' Tamara's voice was a husky disbelieving whisper.

'No, you don't have to go and work for him,' Nigel assured her quickly. 'I've managed to persuade the Board that I can find Zach a perfectly competent secretary without having to do without my own invaluable assistant.'

'But have you managed to convince Zach?'

Nigel fiddled with his pen. 'Not yet,' he admitted, 'but I will do—now don't worry about it.'

That was easier said than done. Tamara worried all through the oppressive, sultry day, which ended without the promised thunderstorm, the dying sun turning the sky a dull brassy gold.

The weekend dragged by with no let-up in the weather. Tamara spent Sunday in the park, telling herself that the fresh air would do her good, but she returned to her flat feeling listless and head-achy. Ever since she had learned that Zach had tried to force Nigel's hand she had been wondering whether she ought to give up her job. She had enough money to tide her over well until after the baby's birth, but her savings wouldn't last for ever, she reminded herself, and she would be lucky to find another boss as understanding and as flexible as Nigel.

By Monday she was no closer to a decision. Thunder was forecast again, but there had been so many false alarms, and the sky was such a heavy, intense blue that Tamara disregarded it, choosing to wear a pretty pink and white striped sundress with a matching white belt, a short-sleeved cotton jacket adding a touch of formality in keeping with the office while still enabling her to keep cool.

Nigel didn't arrive until ten o'clock and quite plainly had things on his mind. Tamara busied herself with her own work, a tiny thread of apprehension coiling in the pit of her stomach, and tightening slowly but surely as the day wore on.

At one she went out for her lunch. There was a snack bar not too far from the office which she normally patronised, mainly because it was clean and the service was quick.

Although her appetite had improved recently, today she felt totally unable to face any food. Instead she ordered a glass of milk, telling herself that it would be good for the baby.

It was just after a quarter to two when she walked back into the office, her eyes adjusting from the too bright glare outside to the welcome coolness of her office. The door between her office and Nigel's was open and she could hear voices coming from it. Frowning, she picked up her diary. Nigel didn't have any appointments. Just as she was wondering which member of staff was in with him Nigel stopped talking and as clearly as though she had been in the room with them she heard Zach saying forcefully:

'Okay then, but just tell me one thing. Is it true that she broke off her engagement with Mellors when she got back from the Caribbean?'

Tamara moved from her desk to the door on leaden feet, her whole body trembling with reaction. What was Zach doing here asking questions about her? Did he somehow think he could use the information that she was no longer engaged to Malcolm to force her to work for him?

Before she could close the door and blot out the sound of his voice and its effect on her far too vulnerable senses she heard Nigel saying calmly:

'That, I think, is Tamara's business.'

'And you aren't going to let her come and work for me?'

'I'm not going to force her into something she doesn't want to do,' Nigel corrected patiently. 'And before you ask, I have no idea why she doesn't want to, any more than I know why you appear so adamant that she should.'

'No?' The word was loaded with contemptuous disbelief. 'I suppose it would be naïve to ask what you stand to gain by championing her like this?'

'If you mean what I think you mean,' Tamara heard Nigel say evenly, 'then it would be presumptuous rather than naïve. Tamara is my secretary, and a very good one. She is also a very attractive young woman, more so now than at any time in the past, especially since she's managed at last to conquer her own lack of self-esteem and liberate the beautiful girl she's always kept hidden behind a wall of reserve. But as for either of us wanting an affair, you insult us both. I happen to be very happily married—a state I can readily recommend, by the way,' he added with a note in his voice which puzzled Tamara. 'And Tamara . . . Tamara is a girl who still believes in love,' he said obliquely.

Tamara didn't wait to hear any more. Grabbing her bag, she hurried out of the office, unable to endure the prospect of facing Zach and having him browbeat her into returning to the Cotswolds to act as his secretary.

When she got outside she realised that the afternoon had dulled and that ominous clouds had built up on the horizon. She had told the girl on reception that she was going home because she wasn't well, and only hoped that Nigel would understand.

As she hurried through the crowded streets towards her bus stop she could hear the menacing roll of thunder clouds, filling the sky at an almost unbelievable speed. Lightning flared as the afternoon turned dark, huge drops of rain darkening the pavement, and the thunder continued to growl, growing ominously closer.

Tamara wasn't frightened of thunderstorms, but she didn't find them particularly attractive, especially when she was only wearing a thin dress and jacket. By the time she reached the bus stop it was raining in earnest, a heavy downpour that soaked straight through her jacket.

The bus stop was deserted, and Tamara was just in time to see the bus rolling away from her less than a hundred yards down the road. Defeat rounded her shoulders, and she shivered beneath the damp lash of the rain, wishing for the protection of some sort of shelter, but there was none.

Within minutes her dress and jacket were soaked, her fingers damp and cold, as she waited in vain for her bus. Too late she remembered the service was less frequent during the day—one of the cuts imposed by councils anxious to cut down on rates, a step which Tamara approved in theory but which was now proving extremely annoying in practice.

The rain was so heavy that she didn't see the powerful car approaching until it ground to a halt in front of her, and even then she didn't realise what it portended until the passenger door was flung open and Zach leaned across to demand threateningly, 'Are you going to get in voluntarily or do I have to use force? Don't try running, Tamara,' he warned her, when she cast an involuntary and frightened look over her shoulder, 'I'm in no mood to be gentle when I catch you—and I will!'

It was only the knowledge that he spoke the truth—she couldn't outrun him—that made Tamara acquiesce and climb reluctantly into the

Porsche, her wet clothes dripping damply over the soft cream hide seats and the thick pile carpet.

'What . . . How did you know where to find me?' she demanded, already knowing the answer to her original question, which had been, 'What are you doing here?'

'It wasn't difficult,' he told her curtly. 'The receptionist was so alarmed by the way you went rushing out of the office that she came up to tell Nigel. From there it wasn't hard to conclude that you must be heading for home—like any other frightened animal, eh, Tamara?'

She didn't respond to that, keeping her eyes fixed firmly on the pavement, a startled protest breaking from her lips as she realised they weren't heading in the right direction.

'Where are you taking me?' she demanded urgently. 'We're going the wrong way!'

'And it's a road we've been down too many times already,' Zach replied grimly. 'I'm taking you to my flat, Tamara. I want to talk to you.'

'We have nothing to say to one another,' Tamara replied breathlessly. 'I'm not going to work for you, even if it means giving up my job.'

'Did I say I wanted you to?'

The question threw her. If he didn't want her to work for him what was he doing following her? Unless of course he wanted to taunt her with her broken engagement; to challenge her with having overplayed her hand when she 'deliberately allowed herself to become pregnant', to paraphrase his own accusation.

She shivered suddenly, trembling with the onset of cold and fear.

'You're soaking.' A frown touched Zach's eyes briefly as he reached forward to touch a switch and heat began to fill the car. 'What possessed you to run out like that . . . Surely it wasn't fear? Not from a girl who faced possible death so bravely.'

Don't hurt me any more, Tamara wanted to plead, but she folded her lips tightly over the words. She had been humiliated enough—more than enough.

She was so engrossed in her thoughts that she didn't realise they had turned off the main road and were entering an underground car park.

'Where are you taking me?' she demanded again, her eyes registering her fear.

'I've already told you—somewhere where we can talk without being interrupted,' Zach replied briefly, switching off the engine and reaching behind her to remove his jacket from the back seat, the brush of his fingers against her wet arm making Tamara flinch and stiffen.

'Well,' he taunted, 'are you going to get out of your own free will or do I have to carry you?'

It had the effect he had known it must. She stumbled out of the car, swaying slightly with shock and apprehension.

Zach took her arm, propelling her towards a private lift which bore them upwards in a thick silence. An impersonal foyer carpeted in dull gold met Tamara's eyes as the lift stopped and the doors opened. Only one door faced them and Zach motioned her towards it while he produced a key.

A small hallway carpeted in the same gold with two excellent Turner reproductions hanging on the walls opened out into a large living room, with a vast expanse of plate glass window overlooking the City.

The flat was obviously much larger than

Tamara's and she was miserably conscious of her bedraggled appearance, her clothes dripping water on to the immaculate pale grey carpet; chilled by the perfect decor of the room, with its silver grey walls, stark black leather settees, and chrome and smoked glass shelving units. It was the sort of room often featured in glossy magazines, but Tamara found it impersonal and unwelcoming.

Zach had disappeared in the direction of another room, and she gasped as he suddenly reappeared bearing a thick fluffy towel.

'Get those wet things off,' he commanded briskly. 'You're soaked to the skin. You'll be lucky if you come out of this with nothing worse than a bad chill!'

Tamara looked round wildly for the bathroom— anywhere that was private, but Zach was standing over her, his stance subtly threatening, his eyes as alert as a predatory animal's.

'If you'll just tell me where the bathroom is,' Tamara began with chilly dignity.

'Oh, for God's sake!' Zach swore, his expression that of a man driven way beyond the boundaries of his self-control. The towel was flung to the floor, Tamara's whispered protests ignored as knowledgeable fingers peeled off her soaking jacket. Her dress was next, the small buttons dealt with with a ruthless efficiency that appalled her, all her feeble attempts to restrain him shrugged aside as though they were those of a helpless child.

Not until he had removed every single scrap of her clothing did Zach reach for the towel, and then he did not hand it to her, and allow her at least some measure of privacy as she had hoped, but instead started to towel her damp body briskly, rubbing fiery life into limbs which had been chilled to the bone.

Quite when the brisk movements altered and became subtly sensual Tamara couldn't say. One moment she was standing shivering, hating him bitterly, and the next, or so it seemed, her frozen limbs were responding to his touch in a way which was entirely alien; the blood which had seemed like ice in her veins suddenly beating urgently under her skin, carrying with it an age-old message of desire and need. An aching which began in the pit of her stomach spread hungrily to every corner of her body. It was impossible to hide from Zach how she felt; it was there in every pliant line of her body, in the shimmering heat of her eyes, and the soft promise of her mouth. When the movement of his hands ceased and he stood perfectly still she was no more able to prevent the soft protest forced past her lips than she could stop herself from swaying yearningly towards him.

'Tamara!' He said her name thickly, his own eyes mirroring her desire. 'Do you want me?'

'Yes . . . Yes . . .' Her body seemed to have developed a will of its own, completely overriding her mind. She moved towards him, pressing tiny hungry kisses along the line of his jaw and the male warmth of his throat, feeling him swallow and stiffen with feminine triumph as his arms came round her and he swung her up in them.

His bedroom was decorated in blues and greys, coolly masculine, but Tamara was barely aware of the sleek fitted furniture or the thick shag pile carpet. She could feel the coolness of the navy silk bedspread against her skin, and closed her eyes childishly, not wanting to look at Zach and see contempt in his eyes.

Why shouldn't she take what the gods offered? she argued rebelliously with herself. It would be little enough to sustain her through the years.

'Tell me you want me,' Zach demanded arrogantly as he leaned over her, his eyes studying the creamy perfection of her body. 'Tell me,' he insisted when she trembled under the touch of his mouth against her skin, tracing a destructive line from her shoulder to where the curve of her breast began.

'I want you.' It was a husky, broken admission, but it didn't seem to satisfy him, because he gripped her wrists, pinioning them together, his eyes darkening to jade as he demanded softly, 'Don't just tell me, Tamara, show me.'

It was then that common sense should have reasserted itself, should have warned her that there was no way she could touch and caress Zach's body without betraying to him how she felt, but as though her body exulted in playing with fire, her hands lifted to the buttons of his shirt, her lips placing trembling kisses against the flesh she was slowly exposing, her eyes avoiding Zach's and the brooding watchfulness she knew was in them.

When she reached the belt of his trousers she stopped uncertainly. 'Go on,' Zach urged her thickly. 'For God's sake don't stop now. I want to know your touch on every part of me, Tamara,' he whispered against her mouth. 'I want you to remember long after we're apart and other things are forgotten what it felt like to touch me.'

She might have stopped then, appalled by the cruelty she glimpsed deep in his eyes, but the sweetly insistent pressure of his mouth on hers suppressed natural caution and instead she did as he instructed, her fingers trembling uncertainly over hair-roughed male thighs, Zach's suddenly fevered groan finding a response within her own body. Her marauding hands were removed and clamped to his shoulders, his lips beginning a sweetly savage exploration of her breasts, fuller since her pregnancy, and as though he sensed their greater sensitivity his possession of their passion-hardened peaks was tender as well as arousing. It was only when his hand explored the subtly altered swell of her stomach that Tamara felt him stiffen, desire no longer hazing his eyes as his fingers stilled on her gently rounded abdomen, a question in his eyes that made her tremble for her own vulnerability.

'Why didn't you tell Mellors about the baby?' he asked softly.

'I . . .' She was lost for words.

'Did you think he wouldn't marry you? Or did you break off the engagement before you knew? It was just after our return from the Caribbean that you broke it off, wasn't it? Don't lie to me, Tamara,' he insisted, 'I know the truth. You see, Dot Partington wrote to me and her letter contained some very illuminating facts—such as the ending of your engagement. And yet you allowed me to believe it still existed, and even to suggest that you had deliberately become pregnant to force Mellors' hand. Why, I wonder?'

Tamara tried to shrug nonchalantly, a terrible cold fear invading her body. She wanted to get up and run for shelter, but Zach's superior weight kept her pinned to the bed. Her stomach clenched and as though he sensed the movement his fingers tightened.

'The baby's mine, isn't it?' he said flatly.

'I didn't want you to think I held you responsible in any way,' Tamara told him nervously. 'That's why I didn't tell you about breaking my engagement, why I let you believe it was Malcolm's. I was frightened you'd try to force me to have an abortion,' she admitted, voicing for the first time one of her most terrifying fears.

'And you didn't want that?'

Tears filmed her eyes, suspending words. She shook her head.

'So I completely misunderstood the situation, just as I've misunderstood so much. You weren't holding on to your viginity simply because you thought it was a good bargaining counter at all, were you?'

'Malcolm never . . . I . . . I always avoided men who wanted sex,' Tamara admitted baldly at last. 'You see, my aunt—she brought me up—she taught me that nice girls don't like that sort of thing, that . . .'

'It's okay, I get the picture,' Zach interrupted harshly. 'So, you were quite happy with Malcolm, quite content to wait for your wedding night before fulfilling your duties as a wife, and Mellors, damn him, is the type who wouldn't expect you to want pleasure, never mind ensuring that you received it.'

Tamara's skin coloured at his frankness, but she didn't deny what he said.

'So where does that leave us?' he asked at last.

'You mean about the baby?' Tamara looked nervously at him. 'There's no need to worry. I won't ever tell it that you're its father, or expect you to do anything for it. I've got some money and Nigel has promised that I can keep my job.'

'Very noble of him,' Zach sneered savagely, 'but you can tell him to keep his job—I'm perfectly capable of supporting my own child. And besides,' he added gratingly, 'I wasn't referring to the baby—we'll discuss that later. I'm talking about this.'

'This' was the way her nerves shivered in mindless pleasure as he kissed her slowly and expertly, drawing from her a response that shocked and frightened with its abandoned sensuality. 'And this,' he murmured, his tongue trailing fire along her throat and down to where the soft fullness of her breasts thrust urgently against the male warmth of his chest, aroused almost beyond endurance by their contact with his hair-roughened chest.

'Tamara, listen to me,' he said at last, cupping her face and forcing her bewildered pain-filled eyes to meet his. 'I'm not doing this to hurt you, whatever you think now. Hurt you—God,' he swore fluently, 'don't you think it's tearing the guts out of me, being like this with you, knowing ...' He caught himself up and said quietly, 'You already know why I was on St Stephen's. I was trying to come to terms with what had happened in Africa, and the last thing I wanted was my peace of mind shattered by a sexy creature in a minute bikini, whose body drove mine wild, and whose eyes promised innocence combined with the lure of Eve, so I told myself that it was all a deliberate ploy to lead me on, and I kept on telling myself that, all the time ignoring every scrap of evidence to the contrary.

'When we were imprisoned together I told myself it wouldn't make any difference, and that what I felt for you was the result of mere propinquity, but propinquity, no matter how effective, never drove any man to want to kill another simply for looking at a woman. Do you remember when we escaped from the caves?'

'Yes.' Tamara shuddered. 'That man ...'

'I knew that was our only chance of escape, but you'll never know what it cost me to force you to do it. I think I knew then, not only how innocent you were, but that I was falling in love with you, but I wouldn't admit it, instead I punished you for daring to breach my defences, albeit completely unwittingly.

'Even when I took your virginity.' He saw the colour flood up under her skin, and smiled, wryly. 'Not a pleasant memory for either of us, I suspect. One half of me loathed myself for what I'd done, while the other struggled to excuse my behaviour by insisting that you were a shrewd tactician, using your virginity as a bargaining counter.

'I thought I was getting over you when I left you behind in the Caribbean—a cowardly action if ever there was one. Having carried you through that forest in my arms, having lain at your side, bathing your fever-soaked body, I knew I was dangerously close to succumbing completely and begging you to marry me—and then you appeared at the Mellors'. The shock almost drove me out of my mind, especially when I discovered that you were engaged to their son.'

'I broke off our engagement the moment Malcolm returned home,' Tamara told him softly, 'but he persuaded me to pretend we were still engaged just for that weekend. He didn't want to ruin his parents' plans for the weekend.'

'Instead of which he almost discovered me on the point of making love to you,' Zach concluded grimly, his eyes fixed firmly on her soft lips as he added huskily, 'It's a pity he didn't, because if I'd made love to you then I'd never have been able to let you go and we'd have avoided all these weeks of misery and anguish. It was after that weekend that I faced the truth—that I loved you and that you were the innocent you seemed; an innocence I myself had destroyed. I thought you were engaged to Mellors, but I told myself engagements could be broken; I even contemplated telling him the truth, and wiping the smug smile of satisfaction off his face when I told him that I'd possessed you, felt your body quicken with desire—and then came that damned lunch, and I discovered you were pregnant,' Zach said flatly. 'I didn't know what I wanted to do the most—kill you, kill Mellors, or kill myself.'

'I was terrified you would discover the truth; that you would think I was using the baby to force you into a relationship you didn't want, so I let you think it was Malcolm's,' Tamara confessed.

'Even thinking that you were carrying his child didn't alter the way I felt about you. I forced you to come and work for me, but having you so close and yet so distant nearly drove me out of my mind. I wanted to punish you; to have you beg me to make love to you; to have you admit that you cared nothing for Mellors. That afternoon when I came back and found you asleep from exhaustion . . .'

'I wanted you to make love to me then,' Tamara admitted softly, 'but I was terrified of betraying how I felt about you, and then there was Julie . . .'

'An old friend,' Zach shrugged her aside as unimportant. 'I admit that I did put her up to it, in the hope that she might make you jealous.'

'Well, you certainly succeeded,' Tamara told him wryly.

'I could have throttled Mellors when he damn near let that horse savage you. I wanted to ask him if he cared the slightest about you or your child.'

'I was terrified you would say something to him,'

Tamara admitted, 'I was so thankful to see Nigel.'

'Yes, so I noticed.'

'It wasn't very fair of you to go to the Board over his head,' Tamara reproached him.

'I was a man in love, and as such fairness never entered into it. When I received Dot's letter, I could hardly believe my eyes. What did I think of you breaking your engagement? she asked me.'

'I heard you asking Nigel about it,' Tamara admitted. 'I was terrified that once you knew the truth about my engagement you'd put one and one together, and . . .'

'Come up with three?' Zach suggested softly, his eyes smiling as he glanced at the soft swell of her stomach.

'Zach, you don't have to feel responsible . . .' she began uncertainly. 'You . . .'

'Why the hell not?' Zach demanded. 'I am responsible, I want to be responsible.' His voice shook suddenly. 'Tamara, haven't you the faintest idea of how it makes me feel to know that that's my child growing inside you; to know that no other man has ever touched you or known you as I have? It's primitive and old-fashioned, and if you'd asked me six months ago I'd have said I didn't give a damn about virginity and certainly never expected it in my wife—and I still think it's morally wrong for any man to expect a standard of behaviour from a woman that he hasn't held to himself, but as I said, taking you, knowing that I was the first, teaching you to respond to me, touched something elemental deep inside me, inside most men, I suppose; something that goes way beyond civilisation and logic. I love you,' he whispered huskily, 'and I can't think of anything my life has held that means more to me than loving you. That first time,' he said abruptly, changing the subject. 'If I hurt you . . .'

'Fleetingly,' Tamara told him. 'And I wanted you so badly it didn't matter.'

'And the baby?' Zach pressed, anxiety lying at the back of his eyes.

'Can't you guess? He's the most important thing in my life,' Tamara teased, adding quickly, 'After his father, of course.'

Her muscles contracted as Zach bent his head to kiss her rounded belly; all that was feminine and instinctive within her rising up to meet the sensual promise of his touch.

'Mine,' Zach murmured slowly, and Tamara knew he wasn't merely referring to the life she held cradled within her. 'You realise, of course, that his arrival is likely to arouse a certain amount of speculation and gossip?'

Tamara shrugged. 'Lots of couples don't marry these days . . .'

'But we aren't going to be among them,' Zach told her flintily. 'What I meant was that his arrival so speedily after our marriage will be talked about. We won't even be able to pretend he's premature.'

'I don't care,' Tamara told him, amazed to realise that it was perfectly true. 'I'm not ashamed of what happened between us; it was the most beautiful thing in my life, and I treasured it because I knew I would never experience it again.'

'Then you knew wrong, didn't you?' Zach told her throatily, drawing her down against him and letting her feel the aroused heat of his desire. 'As I'm going to prove to you just as soon as you promise me that you'll marry me as soon as it can be arranged.'

'And if I don't?' Tamara teased,

She felt him draw slightly away, his eyes darkening. 'If you don't then it will be a solitary memory,' he told her flatly. 'I want you as my wife, Tamara, as the mother of my children—not someone to share the odd night of pleasure with. I want all or nothing, so which is it to be?'

Her open arms and shining eyes gave him his answer, and as his arms tightened around her Tamara gave herself up to the fierce pleasure of his possession, knowing for the first time that it was born of love.

A TINY FEATHERED FRIEND

The hummingbird is a favorite midsummer's guest in anyone's garden, and it is so curious it might well seem to be a miniature creature of imagination visiting from some distant fairyland!

Often seen on hot July afternoons, this tiny bird is sometimes no larger than a bumblebee, with wings like blurs of gossamer fluttering as fast as ninety times a second—thus making the humming sound that gives the bird its name. A hummingbird can hover in midair, its long thin beak extended into the center of a flower to draw out nectar and tiny insects with its tubular tongue. When it has finished feeding, the hummingbird has the unusual ability to fly backward, withdrawing its beak from the flower and darting off to new adventures.

A hummingbird's nest, made of pieces of straw woven together with spiders' webs and decorated with bits of green lichen, is only about as big as a person's thumb; usually it contains just two very small eggs. The mother hummingbird fights valiantly to keep intruders away; but the vividly colored male, with feathers of iridescent green, red or blue, cares little for family life, preferring instead to fly about the garden. If he's feeling particularly lazy, he might feed on honey or sugar water at special red bird feeders built by some homeowners solely for the pleasure of the tiny hummingbird.

Despite their minute size, these birds are quite hardy. The ruby-throated hummingbird, which is the most common species in eastern North America, has been known to fly nonstop all the way across the Gulf of Mexico—a distance of almost 1,000 miles!

Legacy of
PASSION
BY CATHERINE KAY

A love story begun long ago comes full circle...

Venice, 1819: Contessa Allegra di Rienzi, young, innocent, unhappily married. She gave her love to Lord Byron—scandalous, irresistible English poet. Their brief, tempestuous affair left her with a shattered heart, a few poignant mementos—and a daughter he never knew about.

Boston, today: Allegra Brent, modern, independent, restless. She learned the secret of her great-great-great-grandmother and journeyed to Venice to find the di Rienzi heirs. There she met the handsome, cynical, blood-stirring Conte Renaldo di Rienzi, and like her ancestor before her, recklessly, hopelessly lost her heart.

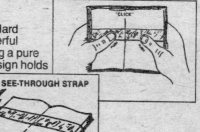

SUPERROMANCE

Longer, exciting, sensuous and dramatic!

Fascinating love stories that will hold
you in their magical spell till the last page
is turned!

Now's your chance to discover the earlier
books in this exciting series. Choose from
the great selection on the following page!

Choose from this list of great

SUPERROMANCES!

SUPERROMANCE

Complete and mail this coupon today!

- -

Worldwide Reader Service

In the U.S.A.
1440 South Priest Drive
Tempe, AZ 85281

In Canada
649 Ontario Street
Stratford, Ontario N5A 6W2

Please send me the following SUPERROMANCES. I am enclosing m
check or money order for $2.50 for each copy ordered, plus 75¢ to
cover postage and handling.

☐ # 8	☐ # 14	☐ # 20
☐ # 9	☐ # 15	☐ # 21
☐ # 10	☐ # 16	☐ # 22
☐ # 11	☐ # 17	☐ # 23
☐ # 12	☐ # 18	☐ # 24
☐ # 13	☐ # 19	☐ # 25

Number of copies checked @ $2.50 each = $_____
N.Y. and Ariz. residents add appropriate sales tax $_____
Postage and handling $_____.7_
           TOTAL $_____

I enclose _____ .
(Please send check or money order. We cannot be responsible for cas
sent through the mail.)
Prices subject to change without notice.

NAME_____
                      (Please Print)
ADDRESS_____ APT. NO._____
CITY_____
STATE/PROV._____
ZIP/POSTAL CODE_____

Offer expires August 31, 1983   3025600000